The Bayou Privilege

THE BAYOU
PRIVILEGE

Dallari Landry

Dallari Landry

CREATIVE ARTS BOOK COMPANY

BERKELEY • CALIFORNIA

For information contact:
Creative Arts Book Company
833 Bancroft Way
Berkeley, California 94710
(800) 848-7789

ISBN 0-88739-354-3 Paper
ISBN 0-88739-356-X Cloth
Library of Congress Catalog Number 00-103032

Printed in the United States of America

Dedication

for Louis and Michael

Acknowledgments

In writing this book, I was encouraged and supported by my dear friend June Johnson. She carefully steered me through the maze of the human mind with her background in psychology, and even proofread the manuscript. There's no one quite like her.

Thanks to Sharon McDonald, friend and coworker, for her patience, friendship, and talented contribution to *Bayou*'s word processing.

I am deeply indebted to Lynn Park, my wonderful and dedicated editor, who diligently assisted me at every turn and graciously answered my questions.

My lovely mother, Johnnie Landry, painted the beautiful oil that was reproduced as *Bayou*'s cover. I have always been in awe of her presence and talent, and I love her dearly.

A heartfelt thanks to you all.

THE BAYOU PRIVILEGE

Privilege:
A special right or advantage granted to one person or group
Information that need not be disclosed in a court of law

Chapter One

$\mathcal{H}$e was pale, his eyes glassy and bloodshot. Wayne looked as if he were keeping a secret. I had never seen him with his hair disheveled or without his cowboy hat. It hurt to see him this way, and I was glad that Anna was not here.

She loved his wit, his crude sense of humor, and most of all his company. Yes, it's best that she wasn't home when I called her to join me. I stood motionless for several minutes. I was in some sort of trance—when the voice of my lab technician jolted me back.

"Are you all right?" Cindy gave me a look of sympathy.

"Yeah, yeah. I'm here now. Let's get to work, it's late."

We had been called away from our beds at one-thirty A.M. to make this forty-mile drive into Presley, a small town not far from the Gulf Coast in the deep piney woods of southeast Texas.

The pathologist entered the small laboratory and gave me a quizzical look. He wasn't certain who we were, what we wanted, or why we were there. It's true that I had no uniform, no lab coat, no readily apparent identification, nothing that would indicate my status as a forensic chemist.

My looks were deceiving as well. I appeared younger than my chronological age. Most people thought I was a high school student. I am of average height, thin, and have a long, thick, brunette mane that falls to the middle of my back. My sense of style, coupled with a warped sense of humor, never gave hints to my profession. I would never have been described as the nerdy laboratory type. Men constantly told me that I was "easy on the eyes," a southeast Texas expression to indicate their approval of my good looks. Nope, this pathologist had no idea who I was. So, I'd have to make a formal introduction and enlighten him.

"We're here from the Liberty County Crime Lab to conduct a crime scene search of the body of Wayne Jeffries." My voice faltered. You see, I had never worked a crime scene where I knew the deceased. The victims had always been strangers, until now. The pathologist nodded and left the room. I retrieved the camera from our crime scene kit, handed it to Cindy, then pointed towards the body.

"Photograph all entry wounds, all exit wounds, and the body in its entirety," I instructed her. "I'll do a gun powder residue test on his hands. Look, the cops even bagged them for us. How thoughtful—and how unusual."

Cindy smiled at me. She had been pretty nervous up to this point. She hadn't known Wayne well, but she knew of him. He had spoken to her a few times when he picked up Anna and me for lunch. Wayne never paid her much attention. He liked pretty ladies, wild and crazy ladies. Cindy was, well, unattractive. She was lanky like a giraffe with dishwater blonde hair, and had an unpredictable personality.

"Where's the gun?" she asked.

"It's at his house with the detectives, we'll pick it up later." I hoped they hadn't handled it. The pathologist's report said that the weapon was a nine millimeter.

As I swabbed his hands and fingers, I noticed that Wayne's flesh felt rubbery. Rigor mortis was setting in. It didn't take long. Human skin becomes tight and hardens around the bones soon after death. I hated touching him, knowing that he was gone, knowing that he had become a piece of evidence in a bizarre murder case. Anna and I had loved going to the horse races in Louisiana with Wayne. He would pick us up in a limo stocked with exotic wines and hors d'oeuvres, and we would be driven just across the Texas border to "watch the ponies run," as he would say.

I noticed that his diamond rings were missing.

As I entered the pathologist's office, I inquired, "I'm sorry to disturb you, but where are Mr. Jeffries' rings?"

"He didn't come in with any rings, ma'am. I do have his clothing, boots, and a hat. Would you like to see those items?"

"Yes, please."

That's odd. Wayne always wore a diamond ring on every finger, except his thumbs. He even wore diamond pinky rings. Yes, he was ostentatious, and he loved to gamble. His weaknesses had been the stock market and the ponies. His coffee distributing business had done well, and he had expanded it recently to include snacks and condiments. His clients included every major restaurant in the state. He had no competition—or did he? The pathologist handed me a large brown paper envelope containing Wayne's clothing. Blood-stained clothing was always packaged in paper, so testing wouldn't be hindered by the additional putrefaction caused by plastic bags.

"May we take his belongings back to the lab for processing?"

"Certainly, I'm finished with them. Please sign this form indicating that I have released them to you."

"All right, and we'll be leaving shortly. Can you give me directions to his house?"

"Yes, let me write them down for you. It's not a difficult drive, but dark, and one wrong turn could have you circling around in the woods until the sun comes up."

I looked at him and responded, "We wouldn't want that to happen."

"No," he agreed, and smiled for the first time since Cindy and I got there. We gathered our equipment after photographing, fingerprinting, collecting trace evidence, and ballistics evidence from Wayne's body. I looked back once more and nodded goodbye to Wayne.

"Thanks for the good times," I whispered.

I couldn't help myself and walked back to the metal table where his body lay, leaned over, and spoke softly in his ear. "I'm so sorry, no one deserves to be shot in the back in their own home—no one. We'll get them, Wayne. Don't you worry. You have a great view now, go watch the ponies."

Cindy watched me, afraid to say anything. We walked back to the lab car in silence. She turned on a flashlight and began reading the directions out loud. Wayne certainly lived out in the sticks. He liked a lot of land around him. I guess no one heard the gun shots that killed him. There wasn't a neighbor within ten square miles.

I wondered who found him. His wife stayed in Dallas a lot, she didn't like remote living and they didn't get along. The drive wasn't very long, and we managed not getting lost. The police department and the sheriff's office were both present at the scene. There were at least a dozen law enforcement units surrounding the house.

Sergeant LeRoy Roberts approached me as I was fetching my crime scene gear from the trunk.

"Who woke you up?"

"Your chief, thank you very much." I retorted.

"It'll be fun. Don't be a grouch. Join the rest of us night owls, and let's get this party on the road. We secured the scene for you, and we have the red carpet all rolled out." He grinned as he watched for my response.

"Hi, Roy," Cindy drooled. She had a crush on him. He was good-looking, I had to admit. We entered Wayne's mansion of a log cabin. He liked a rustic style, yet it was obvious that he leaned toward flamboyant furnishings. Every room was filled with over-sized chandeliers, Venetian mirrors, and animal mounts. There were huge elk heads from Colorado and exotic game mounts from Africa. No little Texas deer mounts in Wayne's house, no siree. I had never been here, he lived too far off the beaten path. Wayne usually stayed at one of his places in town. He liked to drink and party, which precluded him from making that long, dark drive home.

I wandered from room to room and admired the wooden floors, the mosaic tile in the bathrooms, and the overall elegance of each room, in spite of the animal heads. I don't go much for that kind of thing. Roy led us to Wayne's study in the back of the house.

"Who found him?" I asked.

"Unfortunately, it was quite a surprise for the maid."

"Oh."

"How awful," Cindy added. We all nodded.

"I need the murder weapon for ballistics testing." I said. "And where are Wayne's rings? The pathologist said he wasn't wearing any."

"I put the gun in a labeled envelope for you. Here it is on the desk. I bagged his rings, they're in my car for safe keeping. I didn't figure there were any tests you could run on them. They will be kept with the other personal items taken from his body, like his wallet. He sure carried a lot of cash, thousands. There's not much of a crime scene to work. It was a pretty clean job. Wayne was found under his desk, shot in the back three times."

"It looks like a few photographs, some hair and fibers, blood from the floor, and maybe some latent prints may be all we get out of this crime scene, besides the gun," I said.

"It's a nine millimeter," Roy stated.

"That's what the pathologist said. Is there a serial number?"

"Nope. It's been etched off."

"Well, I'll see if I can restore the numbers with nitric acid."

"I hope so. Whoever did this job knew the victim, cornered him in the study, used gloves, did the deed, and left in a hurry, with no interruptions. There was no forced entry."

The floor was chalked off where the body had been found underneath the desk. A pool of blood was leaking into the chalk outline. Cindy photographed the study while I looked for prints, hairs, fibers—anything that might lead us to a suspect. I fingerprinted the desk, the bookshelves, and the light switches. Finally, I crouched down and crawled under the desk. While staring at the wooden floor, I saw a bloody shoe-print, then I closed my eyes for a moment. I could feel him. Wayne was present, he was here. His body was at the morgue, but his spirit was here. With my eyes closed, I visualized a flash of light, the glint of a gun, heard angry voices, and saw the disbelief in Wayne's eyes as he was diving under his desk. I could almost see the killer, still firing away at Wayne. Jerking my head up, I hit it hard underneath the desk. I realized the vision was not real. Maybe I'd inhaled one too many chemicals in the lab.

Chapter Two

Waking up in my bed Thursday morning, I realized that moving back to Liberty might have released old ghosts. The nightmares were becoming more frequent. I thought that I had worked through all of the bad memories once I left for law school. Changing careers, husbands, and cities had seemed to be what I needed. The past thirteen years had been good for me. I found someone I really loved, who loved me back. Our son was the joy of my life. Last but not least the law license hanging on the wall of my new downtown office was a source of pride and accomplishment. But here I was again after all these years, having bad dreams about my old friend. Why did Wayne still haunt me? After his murder, I dreamed about him every night until I moved away. Then after a few months the ghosts seemed to leave.

Last night's awful dream left me nauseated and dizzy. I had to hold on to the nightstand by the bed to steady myself. This was not something I did often, because I was one of the lucky professionals who had not succumbed to drugs or alcohol to hush the voices.

What I was feeling was the direct effect of a recurring nightmare. Everyone has an occasional nightmare, but I had been having this one for months. It was detailed in technicolor and etched forever in my brain. Seemingly real, it was as if someone were reaching out from the dream world to summon me.

I gathered my thoughts and raised myself up off the antique wash stand.

I walked carefully over to the shower on the other side of the room, turned on the water, and waited for it to get warm. It seemed to take forever, and finally I staggered into the shower to clear my head. As the water rushed over my body, I attempted to leave the horrible dream world behind me and return to life.

My morning routine was rushed, and within minutes I backed my new sport utility vehicle out of the garage. My destination was the Liberty County Courthouse, a few miles away. I was contemplating a nice assault case, two driving while intoxicated cases, a criminal mischief, and a nasty divorce, all needing disposition today. I thought about the various cases and what I would do and say when I arrived at the courthouse. Then I called my mother on my digital phone to see about her plans for the week. After that I listened to an Elton John compact disc. "Tiny Dancer" was an old favorite. The CD player shuffled the music of Creedence Clearwater Revival, Led Zeppelin, Billy Joel, Frank Sinatra, and Elvis Presley. My brother Dale always insisted I had weird taste when it came to music.

But I just couldn't get the dream off my mind. I arrived at the courthouse, bounced out of my car in the hyper way that I always did, and entered the old limestone edifice. Courthouses always gave me the creeps, no matter how many of them I entered and departed. They were all eerie and foreboding. Some of the usual suits were huddled around their clients, while others were having coffee and telling jokes or spilling the latest gossip. I found my clients, sat down with each one, and explained again why we were here today. The bailiff and the judge entered the courtroom, and after the bailiff announced, "All rise," we rose, then sat back down.

The judge called the docket. As I watched him I reflected back on his background and that of other judges and their different styles and personalities. This was Judge B, one of our retired judges, a visiting judge. He enjoyed talking about every woman who entered the courtroom: prosecutors, defense attorneys, jurors, court reporters, any and all of the female gender who came before him. I had been told early on not to get on the elevator with him if I was alone, because he was a notorious groper. I thought it was funny. I never really worried about it, although he had groped me at a political fundraiser, right in front of his wife, who appeared to be over-medicated. I just walked away feeling tickled.

Judge B used to tell amusing anecdotes and stories. A man committed several murders. Judge B sentenced him to two life sentences, which were to run consecutively, meaning that the man would serve about 200 years in the state penitentiary. During the sentencing phase of the trial the defendant expressed concern to the judge. His exact words were, "Judge, I just don't think I can do all that time." Judge B whispered back, "Just do the best you can."

I was waiting for my cases to be called so I could respond to the judge as to the disposition and time that each case would take. The judge called the civil docket first, then the criminal docket. Since I had cases on both dockets, I stayed in the courtroom while both dockets were announced. The judge called what we fondly referred to as the "rocket docket," because it went so fast. If you were on the judge's bad side, you would be on "total recall" instead of just recall, meaning you could spend the entire morning, and probably the afternoon as well, waiting for your case to be heard.

While in his court, I tried to be diplomatic, capable, and respectful. This morning I got a deferred adjudication for the client in my assault case, meaning he would be on probation but have no conviction. Not a bad outcome for a guy who hit his cousin in the head with a shovel. My driving while intoxicated cases were set for trial in one month. The criminal mischief case was dismissed. My divorce client sat sobbing quietly, even though she was the one who filed for the divorce that was finally settled today. I left the courthouse with the same mixed feelings of remorse and regret that I always have after finalizing divorce cases. Both sides of a divorce suffer, even if the results are favorable to one party. As for the children, they suffer no matter who gets custody.

After ten years in practice I still questioned myself, "Did I do a good job? Did I do what was in my client's best interest? Could I have done anything differently, or could the outcome have been better? Did I pass the test?" I've always been afraid of failing tests.

Chapter Three

I drove fast and furious back to the office. I never drive the speed limit. I just can't do it. In a prior life, I must have been a male NASCAR driver—male because of the sense of entitlement. That's how I drive. I've been stopped by the cops lots of times, but I haven't gotten too many tickets. I used to whip out my crime lab identification card when the red lights began flashing in my rear-view mirror. Those were my forensic chemist days, before I became a lawyer. The identification looked like something issued by the FBI. Most of the time cops would let me go or, recognizing me, wave me on. A lot of times I had an intoxilyzer in the back of the car. That's the instrument law enforcement officers use to test the amount of alcohol in someone's lungs. Along with investigating crime scenes, analyzing evidence, and testifying in court, maintaining the intoxilyzer had also been part of my job at the crime lab. Once a cop would see it, he would cut me loose to speed on my way. Once a state trooper actually apologized for stopping me, as if I were a fellow officer. But cops see attorneys differently from the way they see crime lab personnel. They considered "official" crime workers to be one of them, on the same side, so to speak. On the other hand, police officers resented lawyers, whose basic courtroom duty was to "grade their papers."

Lawyers pointed out sloppy police work, made them look stupid, and scrutinized every move they made during a trial.

Here he comes, deputy dog, defender of the roadways, a lawyer-hating cop, because I am speeding in a big way. Look at that, a big smile from Officer Roberts. Who would've thought undercover cop LeRoy Roberts, a.k.a. Roy, would be working a speed trap like a traffic cop? I returned the smile and snapped, "What the hell are you doing out here, Roy?"

"Well, I recognized your car and I just wanted to talk to you. I'm out here waiting for a warrant related to a drug bust down old Ranch Road 12. Remember the good old days, when we used to be on the same side of the law and worked cases together?"

Roy looked good. He had gotten grey early, but it suited him. Still tall and slim with mischievous blue eyes.

"Yeah, I remember when you resented me for being accepted to law school when you couldn't get in. After all, I was just a woman. You thought that only men should be lawyers. I also remember when we were dating, and you screwed my lab technician. How could I forget such lovely fucking memories?"

"Damn, you still holding that grudge?"

"With both hands. I'm a little pissed that you're still abusing your position. What authority do you have to detain me? You pulled this bullshit with me years ago. Don't prosecutors call this 'official oppression'?"

"I only wanted to see you because I knew you were back in town. I know you never liked me jumping out of the car when we were on a date, chasing down criminals, and calling in on the police radio. But, if I hadn't taken this opportunity today, you could have avoided me forever."

"I should hope so. My downfall has always been that I have very high standards and expectations."

"I'm sorry I stopped you. It won't happen again. I promise."

"I'll have to accept that even though I know your word isn't worth squat." Roy ignored my insult.

"Why don't you join me on the bust? You know everyone who's going to be there. Drug Enforcement Agency is in full force, Department of Public Safety is sending Pagden, and all the usual guys from Liberty County sheriff's office will be there. The police department has every undercover cop on the payroll there; even the Texas Rangers are en route as we speak. Do it for old times sake. It'll be fun."

"I remember your definition of fun. Your idea of fun is poking your nose into people's private lives. Evidently, you haven't read the amendments to the Constitution. When I first became a chemist at the crime lab, you researched my background until you came up with my name: Michelle Marie Monroe. You found out that I was twenty-three years old and a recent college graduate with a B.S. in biology and chemistry. You also had my academic transcript and my LSAT score— and you didn't stop there. You found out that my father worked for the Texaco refinery, that my mother was a housewife with an artistic talent, and that I had three brothers. As a matter of fact, you even knew that I had married and divorced my high school sweetheart. Need I go on?"

"No, but can't you forget all of that for once? You won't be sorry, and everyone will be glad to see you."

"What if I miss a potential client because of this deal? You know that making the scene will mean a conflict, and I wouldn't be able to take any case that might arise from this alleged crime. How many arrests are possible?"

"Well, we're really after one guy, a really big guy. You know him, so you wouldn't be able take the case anyway."

"Who?"

"Your old boss."

"No way!"

"Yep, we've been working this case since you left, and it's pretty big. Let's just say that it goes way beyond drugs, sex, and rock and roll. The only way you'll find out more is to come with me and watch the investigation in progress."

"Let me call the office and switch my appointments around because now you've got my curiosity going."

Chapter Four

I got on my digital phone and called Sherry at the office to have her reschedule my afternoon appointments for the next morning. Then I followed Roy to a remote location just outside a small town named Starks. We had been driving for about thirty minutes when I saw some familiar looking landmarks. Though I had never been out this way before, it did elicit a feeling of déjà vu.

When we finally passed an empty farm house, I saw an emerald green '67 Pontiac Firebird abandoned just beyond the house. In college I had one that looked just like it. There was a grove of pecan trees and some old headstones near the house. The trees were huge, probably over a hundred years old. Some of the head stones had been recently overturned. I proceeded on, following Roy to our unknown destination.

As we were pulling off the road, it hit me. I had seen the old farm house and the Firebird in a dream I had several months ago. I was spending the night at my parents' house on Christmas Eve, before I moved back to town. In my dream, my mother, my father, my youngest brother, and I all had shotguns. We waited out in the woods hoping to get a shot at a family with whom we'd been feuding. It was a Hatfields and McCoys dream. We were all dressed in camouflage, tiptoeing around, attempting to hide in the bushes.

It was similar to other dreams I'd had in the past. They always involved my immediate family, but were bizarre and reeked of dysfunction. When we were small children I felt loved and protected. But as we grew up, it seemed we had too many distinct personalities living under the same roof. My three brothers were constantly at war with each other and the women in their lives. I was forever defending my siblings. Most holidays drug up latent family issues, though we loved each other dearly. When someone attacked one of us, we all jumped in to help. Unfortunately, we were all very emotional and easily humiliated by nasty scenes. We were left with bittersweet memories of most holidays.

I have never understood my dreams. Now, I've had two very disturbing nightmares. One about my best friend, Jean. And now Wayne's ghost coming back last night. I hope this doesn't mean I'm going to have a lot of weird dreams. I almost rear-ended Roy as he pulled off the side of the road. Why the hell was he stopping? This better not be one of his bullshit stunts. I got out of my car and yelled, "Okay, what are we doing here?"

"Follow me a little further, we have to hide our cars."

Here we go, cloak-and-dagger Roy. What will it be next? I supposed he was right about hiding our cars, if he was on the level about this crime scene. When I was a chemist, I used to be afraid that our marked crime lab car, the one with all the official-looking decals, would get us shot one day by drug dealers who would come home to find their homestead invaded by law enforcement.

All the time I was asking myself, why would I leave my law office on a day with so many clients scheduled? It's not me: I'm organized, meticulous, and responsible. I've let Roy interrupt my schedule. Could it be that I want to spend time with him, despite the old grudge I hold?

After driving a few feet, Roy pulled off the road and continued on through a field of wildflowers. I realized that I had absolutely no idea where we were. Roy drove into a wooded area and parked his car behind a grove of pecan trees, indicating that I do the same.

I got out of my car. "Under no circumstances will I leave here after dark without an escort. Is that understood, super-narc?"

"Loud and clear, and I'll personally return you to where I found you. Is that satisfactory?" Roy was definitely pleased that I had agreed to participate in his little adventure.

"Yes, and I'll stop busting your balls today for the sole purpose of investigating this case. This better be as good as you seem to think it is."

"It's to die for. Well, some people think so anyway."

"What do you mean by that?"

"You'll see if you stick around long enough."

"Well, let's get to the scene. I still have a lot of work to finish before tomorrow morning."

We began walking further and further into the woods. Finally we came to a small boat docked in a swamp. Roy told me to get in. What a creepy-looking, mosquito-infested bayou. I couldn't believe he expected me to get into that tiny-ass row boat.

"For goodness sake, where are we headed—and how much further?"

"Just a few miles by boat."

What had I gotten myself into? Although I didn't trust Roy as a lover, he was a good detective with an admirable record.

"You'll be happy that you came. Your old compadre is going to be there."

I couldn't help feeling a little creepy. I suspected that there were alligators bigger than this boat lurking nearby, waiting for a fresh body to feed on. I've seen them cross the interstate from the bayous near my house, and those guys are huge. I didn't say a thing for the next ten minutes. Because all I could do was look at the eerie surroundings. Moss was hanging in long tendrils, and I was afraid that the insects buzzing in and around the moss were going to drop off into the boat. These bugs were big enough to saddle and ride. We hit a few stumps along the way, and Roy had to restart the engine a few times. Man, was that reassuring! After all, who would find us out in the middle of bum swamp USA? No one even knew where I was—not my office, not my family, no one.

That reminded me that I needed to call my best friend, Jean Bug. I've called her that since we met during our first year of college in introductory chemistry. She sat down in front of me the first day of class, turned around, and proclaimed, "I hope this class is all memorization. Chemistry is not my thing." This was before she even introduced herself.

I was tickled and felt obliged to introduce myself. We had similar likes and dislikes, in addition to the fact that both of us were majoring in biology. Jean was minoring in psychology and in later years classified me as a type A personality.

"You are anal retentive and I am anal expulsive."

"What does that mean?" She went into a long psychological explanation that I couldn't understand.

"Whatever, let's talk about something we both love, like Elvis," I urged.

We were both Elvis fanatics. We loved him, his gyrating hips, and his earthy music. Jean had seen him lots of times in concert. I hadn't been as lucky.

This morning I was calling Jean so someone would know where to look for my body if I didn't come back. I was going to call her when I woke up, but she's a real night owl, and I left so early for my court appearances that I hated to wake her. I would have felt foolish waking her up just to tell her that I had bad dreams. I took my digital phone out of my purse and began to dial her number. Roy asked, "Who are you calling?"

"Jean. I want somebody to know where to look for our bodies if we never return, but I'm not sure if I know where the hell we are."

"Jean, it's me. Pick up."

Jean answered in a croaky voice. "What's wrong?"

"Nothing really. I had some scary nightmares. I couldn't quite tell in the dream that I had about you if you were dead or alive."

"Have you had another bad dream like the one you had at your folks' during the holidays?"

"Several. They're like scary short stories, and I don't know what to think about them. This one was much worse because the victim was you. You were dressed to kill in a multicolored silk blouse and skirt. You were wearing high heels and running away from an attacker with a handgun. Several shots were fired."

"Since we're dreaming, can I be skinny with the grace of a

gazelle?" Jean teased. "I'm still here, but I'll be careful. My niece's ex-husband still hates me for outing him, so I guess that I do have at least one enemy. By the way, where are you? You sound like you're in the bottom of a barrel."

"Even worse. I'm in a pirogue with Roy heading for an unknown crime scene destination. If I don't make it out of here alive, I want you to be the one to tell my parents and Les."

"You've got to be kidding."

"I'll tell you about it this weekend. Are we still antique hunting in Shelby?"

"Absolutely."

"Jean, Roy says 'hi'."

"Hi back at him. I always did like him in spite of my natural distaste for authority figures, but I didn't care for his cheapskate, cheating side."

"I had to reschedule my afternoon because of this field trip with Roy so I probably won't call you until tomorrow night. Pack light. We won't need much. Bring a bottle or two of Piesporter, or as my mother refers to it, Pissporter. It's a dry county. I'll pick you up."

"I'll be waiting. Be careful."

Roy didn't miss a beat. "How long have you two known each other?"

"Basically, all of our adult lives. I've been with her through both our divorces, the death of her parents, and just about everything else. She's the best person I know.

"What about you? Who do you hang out with now?"

"No one really, not since you've been gone."

"Are you forgetting that you got married again after I left for law school?"

"It didn't work out, and I don't think about it if I can help it."

"But you do think about your children from that marriage, don't you?"

"You know I do. And I guess that's who I hang out with. I try to spend as much time with my kids as I can. Everyone at the department is busy with their own lives. They don't seem interested or don't have the time to include me in their plans."

"I know. It seemed like it was easier to make friends when we were younger. I think we mature and develop more selective tastes as we discover who we are."

"Still the philosopher, M&M?"

"If I have to be."

Chapter Five

"*O*ur destination is just around the bend."

"It's about time, dude."

An incredible sight came into view. Directly in front of us a white-painted antebellum mansion harked back to the era when cotton was king. Deep verandahs cast cool shadows that echoed the moss cascading to the ground from old oak trees. Formosa azaleas were in bloom as far as the eye could see. There was a gazebo near the back of the house, a generous servant's quarters, a barn, and a stable. I felt as if I were stepping back in time. How could such an ugly, menacing swamp yield such magnificence?

Before I had time to admire anything else, I heard a shout. "Micki, it's my Micki!" There she was, my other best friend in the whole world. I should have called Anna months ago, when I returned to town. I felt foolish because I hadn't, but it didn't seem to matter, because Anna ran toward me with outstretched arms. "How are you?" she crooned in her lovely Loretta Lynn voice.

"I have missed you so much. I'm sorry that I haven't called you, but the move was a difficult one."

She graciously accepted my apology and fast-forwarded our conversation. "How did Roy find you?"

"He ambushed me after court this morning."

As we walked toward the house, Anna gave me the details on the crime scene. "You know just about everyone here today: Charlie, Frank, Hascal, Bert, Steve. I could use your help on this one. As usual, there's no one but me at the lab to work the scene today. One of the technicians is having trouble with her diabetes, the secretary is menopausal today, the chemist is testifying in court, and you know how Bob is always absent when you need him." (I wondered if she knew Bob was the subject of the investigation. Should I mention it?)

Anna went on, "It seems kind of hush-hush. No one's talking. At first glance it appears to be a big drug bust. Can you believe the boat ride out here?"

"What happened to the road?" I asked.

"A hurricane washed it out years ago. They never rebuilt it. Why should they? There's no one living out here."

"What lab supplies did law enforcement request? That may give us some hints."

"They asked for the super glue and the fuming tank, amido black, ninhydrin spray, the laser, drug field screening kits, luminol spray, slides, scalpels, set up for DNA, a comparison microscope—you name it. It took me over an hour just to load this stuff into the lab car."

"Boy, that runs the gamut. Roy told me they're after your boss. What do you know about that?" (I decided to confide in her.)

"Well, it was just a matter of time before they investigated him. His drinking problem has just gotten worse since you left. They may suspect that he's using the lab for his own personal addictions, booze and drugs. The boys' club believes in a very selective dissemination of information. Let's see what we can piece together."

"First, I want to ask the boys how they feel about a defense lawyer working with them. Although Roy thinks it's cool, you know how law enforcement hates lawyers."

"Everyone is in the stables, follow me. I'm told that's where the action is."

As we walked toward the back of the marvelous old house, I asked Anna, "Who owns this place?"

"No one really lives here anymore, but they say that this house has been in Bob's family for over a hundred years. Everything inside the house is covered up, but you can see some wonderful antiques through the windows. Maybe we can get a closer look when the supplemental search warrant gets here. We're supposed to get started inside the stables and the barn. That's all this search warrant covers."

"It's funny that Bob never mentioned this old place."

"It's a real pain in the ass to get here, and Bob never troubles himself for anything or anyone. Supposedly he paid the taxes and sent someone out every now and then to check on the place. Aren't the grounds beautiful? It is so amazing that everything looks so good when it's been virtually neglected for years. Here we are. Wow." Anna's dark eyes were taking in her surroundings. Her black hair was blowing in the spring breeze. I had forgotten how pretty she was. Standing all of five feet tall, she had enormous presence.

"What a huge stable. Look at all of the old equipment and tools. I've seen a lot of this stuff in antique stores and warehouses." I had inherited a fascination for antiques from my parents.

Across the stables near the back door I saw several cops hovering over a large old trunk. As I approached, Charlie, a detective, yelled out, "Look who's here—our long-lost chemist." Most of the guys rushed over to greet me. I was truly honored by this show of affection. After all, I did switch sides when I left for law school, and I never got the chance to say good-bye to any of the people I had worked with for years. I got my letter of acceptance, and in a week I was gone to find an apartment and matriculate among those selected to attend St. Mary's University School of Law in San Antonio.

"It's great to see all of you. I must say that I've missed some of you—and at times I've even missed this gruesome work! Do any of you have a problem with me working this crime scene? So, while we're investigating this case, am I exempt from your general disgust with lawyers?"

"Aw, come on, Micki. You know that we think of you as one of us, and we always will," said Steve, one of the younger deputies. Steve had been with the sheriff's office since he graduated from high school. He was already well respected and had a nose for law enforcement.

"Does everyone feel that way? Charlie? Hascal?"

All nodded, and Hascal, my favorite Texas Ranger, said, "It's okay with us, Micki. You're like family." He was not the most handsome man I ever met, but he was one of the sweetest.

"All right, there's no turning back now. I'll get to work. I see that someone has marked off the areas of interest, and the crime scene has been secured. Anna has been teaching you well."

"Why are you working this case?" asked Steve. "Is it related to the pending investigation of your old boss?"

"Let's just say that Anna needed some help, and I was all she could find."

Steve replied, "I'm sure Pagden won't mind. He's in charge today. He always said you were a hell of a lot better-looking than Bob McNamara."

Anna interrupted this lovefest. "Come on, guys. Let's get busy. We have to finish the stables and barn while we still have some light. I for one am not leaving this alligator-and-snake-infested bayou after dark."

We all began our various tasks. The DEA guys sniffed for drugs with their trained dogs, the cops searched through boxes and trunks, the sheriff's office sprayed amido black on shoe-prints and made casts with plaster of paris, while two Texas Rangers watched and supervised. Hascal was telling cajun jokes and entertaining the others, who were hard at work. He began with the vasectomy joke where the unwitting Frenchman used an empty Coke can and a cherry bomb, then counted to ten. He followed with "How does a cajun eat a frog?" His response: "One leg over each ear." Of course all of the guys roared with laughter.

"Holy shit!" Anna shrieked as she opened an old trunk that had been buried under some horse saddles and riding parapher-nalia. She began pulling what appeared to be human remains from the trunk. It was difficult to say how many different skele-tons were in the trunk. Everyone stopped what they were doing and gathered around Anna and the trunk full of bones. The over-all tone of the crime scene shifted from amusement to the macabre. It was now truly a crime scene, with remains of real human beings. It would be up to the coroner to determine exactly how many people these remains belonged to. We labeled all the bones and then placed them carefully in the containers Anna brought from the lab.

No one spoke until the trunk was empty. Finally Pagden, the superior DPS officer, spoke. "Everyone back to your respective assignments. This may be only the tip of the iceberg."

Anna and I looked at one another. We both suspected he was right.

Anna and I had always worked well as a team. She photographed inside the barn, outside the barn, and the stable areas. She had attended photography training at the FBI Academy in Quantico. She was a champion at utilizing incidental light, and knew how to position the camera to get the best possible picture. This was in great contrast to Bob, who was well known for trying to photograph crime scenes with no film in his camera. He would've threatened our lives if we'd screwed up like that on a high-profile case. He was usually drunk by the time the sun went down, and since most crimes occurred at night, he was generally incompetent to handle any crime scene.

I had always been good at gathering physical evidence and preserving it under the most difficult of circumstances. The gathering and preservation were half the battle, but the ultimate test was the actual forensic results that would eventually lead to the courtroom. My other talents lie in mixing chemicals for testing and in microscopic examination of specimens. I had looked at everything under a microscope, including spermatozoa, paint chips, fibers, hair, glass, bullets, marijuana—you name it.

I was studiously scraping a blood stain from the trunk when Anna asked, "How does your dad like your being a lawyer?"

"He's glad to have me back in town, especially now that he gets to see Michael. He guesses I hang out with a better class of creeps."

Anna completed her photographing. "He didn't like the idea of you working at the crime lab any better than he liked you working around all of those men at the refinery, did he?"

"He didn't mind my being a lab technician at a plastics plant. You have to start somewhere. What he did mind was me being a young woman working around hundreds of middle-aged men. After listening to all his griping and after a year of working overtime and twelve-hour days, it was a relief to find an eight-to-five job—or so I thought. Then you and I wound up working around the clock at the crime lab for almost five years. For him the depravity of the crime scene was even worse than the middle-aged men. But let's go see what the others are coming up with and how much longer they think we'll be here."

"All right. I have all of the photos I need, the bones have all been labeled, and most of the trace evidence has been gathered, thanks to you. What do you have other than blood scrapings?"

"Well, believe me, you have plenty to take back to the lab. There are hundreds of hairs, lots of fibers, a few bullets, some blankets, several old guns, paint scrapings—a real collection. But, I thought that we were looking for drugs."

"That's what I thought too, but so far I haven't found any drugs, ledgers, large sums of money or any of the other drug-related paraphernalia."

"I think they're keeping us in the dark on purpose. How can we be effective if we don't even know what we're looking for?"

"Beats me." Anna shrugged.

As we walked through the stables toward the barn, we saw several of the guys running around out back with their guns drawn. I shouted, "Hey, what's happening?"

"Shhh... we heard someone in the woods, and we think we're being watched," said Ranger Hascal.

"Is this all you guys have done for the last two hours, act paranoid while Anna and I were collecting evidence?"

"Well, the house, is locked down pretty tight. We can't search there till we get the supplemental warrant," Charlie said in his official detective voice. "We'll just have to wait until tomorrow and check things out then. Are you ladies ready to leave now?" he asked.

"Let's roll." Anna motioned with her index finger.

As we proceeded to our respective boats, Roy came running across the front yard like a spotted-ass ape. He was red faced, wild-eyed, and dripping with sweat. His gun was drawn.

Roy was usually dapper, even when distressed. I had never

seen him with a hair out of place, and he had a lot of hair. Sometimes he wore it long with a full beard when working under-cover, but he never looked scruffy.

"Someone shot at me behind the house," he gasped.

By now everyone had gathered near the boats. We were look-ing back toward the area where Roy claimed shots had been fired. Ranger Hascal asked Roy if he'd seen anyone, and Roy admitted that he hadn't. But one of the bullets had buzzed close to his left ear and stuck in a tree. Amazingly, Roy had retrieved the slug from the tree before running for protection. He put it in a plastic bag and handed it to Anna.

"Please run ballistics on the caliber," he said.

The shooter must have used a silencer because no one heard any gunfire. Several of the men stayed behind to check out the area where the gunshot occurred. The rest of us headed out, since we had done all that we could without a search warrant for the house. I wouldn't be returning with the crime lab crew tomorrow. I knew once Bob saw the evening news, he wouldn't let me par-ticipate. After all, when I left the lab, I left him. Bob was as ego-centric as a four-year-old, and he saw my leaving as my aban-doning him. It didn't occur to him that I was bettering my life.

I had covered his ass pretty well while I was his employee. Most employers would miss a good worker, but after I left, Bob did nothing but denigrate my character and my performance. I guess drugs and alcohol lead to a fuzzy perception of life and liv-ing. In turn I resented him for being a low life, devoid of com-passion and understanding, completely self-absorbed. God only knows why Anna continued to work for him. She made his cof-fee, picked up his dry cleaning, and paid his child-support. She had worked with him for years. More than once she had said she felt sorry for him. Maybe she had come to feel responsible for him. Maybe she needed him to need her. Or it could have been that he gave her an opportunity to advance in a field in which she originally had no training. I never quite understood it.

Anna and I got into Charlie's boat and headed back to civi-lization. Despite his promise to me, Roy stayed behind to help Pagden and Ranger Hascal canvas the area.

Chapter Six

*O*ur return journey was quiet at first. The only motion in the swamp was the wake left by the boat's small motor. I saw no egrets, no mallards, no snakes, and no alligator bubbles. It was as if they were all in hiding. Anna broke the silence.

"Micki, if I don't have help tomorrow, could you help me search the house?"

"Sure, but I don't think Bob will let me. Anyway, I have to be in the office tomorrow morning to see the clients I neglected today. And I'll be out of town this weekend, but let me know. I don't want you out there alone."

Charlie hadn't said anything.

"Charlie, you've been quiet. What's the matter?" Anna asked.

"I'm just wondering what we're getting ourselves into out here. They send us out here on a wild goose chase and feed us bullshit about drugs. This whole thing seems bogus. Those bones—we never expected anything like that, and then Roy gets chased by a bullet. There's no telling what we'll find in the house. It's liable to get sanitized or burned down before we get back there. I'll certainly be asking some questions when I get back to the department."

Anna and I looked at each other, then at Charlie. I finally said,

"We thought you guys knew what was going on. If you don't, who does?"

Charlie shrugged. "Beats me. The feds didn't tell us much."

"The feds—what have they got to do with anything? I thought that we had every local law enforcement agency known to man represented here today."

"We did, but our instructions were coming from the fucking feds."

"Look what happens every time the feds get involved with anything—Waco, the Davis Mountains incident, the IRS, the postal service. Need I go on? I hate the FBI, I really do. I've got good reasons, don't I, Anna?" I looked to her for moral support.

"Yes, you do." She turned to Charlie. "Micki took the FBI on single-handedly, and lost."

"All those cover-your-ass hypocrites spend their time looking for scapegoats. I would have never stepped foot onto this crime scene ground if I'd known that those lousy SOB's were involved."

"Micki, we haven't seen each other in a long time. What we did today wasn't much fun, but we still make great partners. Just let the FBI issue go...."

"Okay. I'll shut up. What's your schedule like early next week? I'd like to have drinks and dinner one evening. Maybe I'll even cook."

"Any night. Harry is out of town all week doing a marijuana eradication program somewhere in the boonies of east Texas."

"How about Tuesday?

"Sounds good. By the way, what's with Les and Michael?"

"Les is finishing a building project in Denver and won't be back until June. That's the projected completion date anyway, about three months from now. If they aren't back by then, I'll spend the rest of the summer up there. I miss them. I haven't been alone this long since I was single, and I never stayed home back then. You know it's the nature of the beast to keep busy when you're single so that you never have to go home, except to sleep."

"I don't miss those days a bit, but I do miss some of our little escapades. Remember the time we went to happy hour at the Red Carpet Inn, and that guy took the parking space you'd been waiting for? You pulled your little pearl-handled .25 caliber automatic out of your boot and told him to move it. He mouthed off, then you fired a couple of rounds over his head. He was shitting on one heel and kicking it off with the other, but he did move his ass. He screamed out of there, and we never saw him again."

"I wonder why I didn't pull my .38 out of the console. I was kind of crazy back then."

"What do you mean 'back then'? I don't think so. Look around. Where are you, and who are you with?"

"I guess you're right. I could be in my office right now accomplishing what I set out to do this morning, before I let Roy talk me into this shit. I just can't take a dull life. I've got to live with my hair on fire. Jean, who acts as my surrogate therapist, says that I was over-controlled as a child. Supposedly I act wild and crazy because I need to free my spirit from an oppressive upbringing. According to her and Freud, I'm addicted to the relief I get from my wild urges. Besides, my grandma was crazy, and I'm proud to say that she passed her aberrant tendencies on to me—but I'm functional, ha, ha."

Anna laughed. "You may just be schizophrenic—crazy one day, and responsible the next. After all, you are a Gemini."

I frowned at her. "You know I don't believe in astrology."

"It's got to be as reliable as Freud."

"I think not," I said. For a sensible, intelligent woman she had some silly beliefs. I thought so anyway.

"Where are you parked?" I asked.

"I really couldn't tell you, but Charlie can find the car. I followed him up here."

"I'm parked by Roy, but I don't know where either. So let's make a deal: whoever finds her car first helps the other look for her car."

Anna smiled. "You know we wouldn't leave you out here."

I looked at my watch. It was about five thirty. We docked near where Roy and I had gotten in our boat. Where the hell were the cars? It took fifteen minutes to find Charlie's and Anna's cars, then it took another ten minutes to find mine and Roy's. I started my engine and followed Anna, who was following Charlie out of the thick brush. Staying as close as possible to Anna's tail lights all the way back to the interstate highway made me feel more comfortable.

Chapter Seven

*I*t took me over an hour to get home. I hadn't realized that I'd followed Roy that far into the boonies. I pulled into the driveway and hit the garage door opener. I was anxious to get into comfortable surroundings. I'd been feeling unsettled since we found those bones and all that blood back in the barn. I shuddered to think what the house might hold, if they ever got that search warrant.

What was I thinking? I wouldn't be going back there. I didn't want to, even if Bob would let me. When I opened the patio door, my cat, Jorge, leaped in to greet me. At least he was home, no one else was.

I realized I was lonely without Les and Michael. That's probably why I let Roy talk me into this nonsense. Was it just my curiosity about Bob drawing me into this puzzle, or did I miss forensic work? Or did I miss Roy? Or all of the above?

When I was younger, it was simpler not to think, just to act. That led to consequences and excuses, but it was part of being young. Personal growth and maturity had caused me to analyze, belabor, and fret over most of my daily decisions. It was all part of my obsessive-compulsive nature. I just couldn't give up something for something else. Nor could I give up someone for someone else.

I turned on the kitchen light and checked my message machine. I grimaced while playing them back. I decided to ignore all of the messages except the one from Leslie, my sweet husband. I called him back at his Denver apartment.

"Hi, babe. How's it going? Sorry I missed your call."

"You're in late this evening, aren't you Micki?"

I hated long explanations. "I worked a crime scene with Anna today. It's been a long time, but collecting and preserving evidence is second nature, so it all came back."

"I thought you were happy practicing law."

"I am, most of the time. After court this morning LeRoy Roberts talked me into helping out. The crime lab was short-handed today, with an absent director, as usual. It was just a one-time deal. How's my boy?"

"He's great. He loves staying with your cousin Stephanie and her boys during the day. After I get off work we ride horses, hike, fish—whatever his little heart desires."

"It sounds great. I wish I were there. I should have gone with you and Michael, but I was afraid that I wouldn't have a practice to come back to."

"I know."

"Maybe I'll come up in a few weeks and spend a long week-end with the two of you."

"Let me know when, and I'll pick you up at the airport. I'll be the one with the big smile."

After we hung up, I was starving and munched on some left-overs. Then I reviewed tomorrow's case files and ran a hot bath. I was hoping that it would take the edge off my mood.

It was a restless night, and I woke up with a dull headache, the kind you get from sleep deprivation. I hadn't slept well since Leslie and Michael left for Colorado.

Chapter Eight

I arrived at my office to find Sherry waiting for me with a handful of messages.

"Where have you been? Everyone is looking for you."

"It's a long story."

"Your mother called. Your brother Nick is in trouble. Next, the judge's office wants to know if you're ready to go on the Clifford case today. After that, you have several messages from potential clients. I rescheduled the clients from yesterday afternoon to this morning. The first one will be here in thirty minutes. The last appointment is scheduled for eleven thirty, so you can have lunch and get to court by one o'clock. Your pretrial motions are on your desk for proofreading. Will you be needing anything else right away?"

"Sherry, you can never leave me. I'd just die without you."

"I know. I'll buzz you when your first client arrives. You better start returning those phone calls."

"Hi, mom. What's up?"

"My allergies and your father are driving me crazy, but other than that, I'm all right. Nick got put in jail last night. Your dad and I were going to make him wait until this morning, but one of his friends bailed him out. I don't know what we're going to do."

I listened. I couldn't solve their problems but—God how I wanted to.

My three brothers, particularly Nick, were my inspiration for practicing criminal defense. When I handled cases involving young men who reminded me of my brothers, my immediate reaction to their problems with law enforcement was one to become their protectress, a defender of the defenseless. Young men who inadvertently stepped into the glare of law enforcement limelight kept me in practice. I could look a parent in the face and say, "Yes, I kept your son out of the penitentiary and yes, you paid me to do it." I could live with that. And it helped me forget how much the public hated lawyers and how much I hated being associated with men (most of them in general are still men) who wore expensive suits, drove luxury cars, took exotic vacations, and worked all the time. I flipped to the next message and called a woman regarding a divorce. Her husband wanted to leave her for a lingerie model he'd met online—and never seen. I made an appointment to see her next week.

I was plowing through the other messages. One man was just shopping around for a lawyer. One was a jail inmate who didn't have any money, so the judge had appointed me to represent him. Then Sherry buzzed me.

"Mrs. Heller is here. Shall I send her back?"

"Yes. And please return the rest of these calls for me. Set up appointments and find out if they already have a court date. If they have a court date next week, we may need to refer them to another attorney."

"I gotcha."

I met with Mrs. Heller, who was here about a paternity case involving her son, who was a minor, his girlfriend, and the baby his girlfriend was carrying. She was very protective of her son, and insisted that he was not the father of this rather promiscuous girl's child. Mrs. Heller did not bring her son with her to my office today, but merely showed up to sign the contract requesting my legal services and to pay the initial retainer fee. I explained the procedure for paternity testing, which included blood tests for the mother, the alleged father, and the infant. All the testing would be done after the baby was born.

"But how will blood tests help my son?" she asked.

"If none of your son's genetic markers show up in the baby's blood, then he will be excluded as the father. DNA testing to determine paternity has great credibility in court."

"I guess I don't have to understand all the science stuff as long as you do," she said.

I met my next three clients in the conference room so that we could lay out paperwork, discuss and sign various motions and pleadings, and determine trial strategies.

Then Sherry ordered me take-out for lunch: a spinach salad with grilled chicken and a fruit smoothie. My stomach would be growling within a few hours, but I was trying to keep my figure. As I looked at my lunch, I remembered something an old boyfriend used to say: "If I saw this in the desert, I'd step over it." I laughed to myself and ate it anyway. It was supposed to be healthy.

After lunch I walked across the street to the courthouse to meet my client. I had the dubious distinction of representing a young man who had been charged with cruelty to animals, a class B misdemeanor that could get him up to six months in jail and a two thousand dollar fine. Pretty bad consequences for shooting a chicken. Allegedly, he shot his neighbor's guinea hen and was facing prosecution for this so-called heinous act. The defendant and his neighbor had been feuding for years.

I could believe it. I'd heard more than one colorful story about episodes of insanity in the rural part of the county. Lately, my cases had ranged from the ridiculous to the sublime. The lady prosecutor and I didn't agree on what was a serious crime and what was not. In my opinion, crimes involving violence or injury to others should be prosecuted over accidents and less serious offenses. We had been in trial together a lot lately because of her inability to screen weak cases. I left my office at a decent hour for once and drove home to pack for my weekend with Jean.

Chapter Nine

There was a hint of spring in the afternoon air. I drove home through lovely subdivisions of red-brick homes covered with fig leaf ivy. Rockers moved gently in the wisteria-scented breeze, and swings glided on lush back patios lined with sweet-smelling magnolia trees. Large native pecan trees shaded the neighborhoods. Azaleas were thriving and blooming in the humidity of the south. Children were playing outdoors, mothers were gardening and keeping an eye out, and elders were sitting on their porches.

After dealing with unpleasant legal gymnastics all week long, it felt good to see nature and nice people. It's comforting to know that most people would never need a lawyer, be disappointed in the judicial system, or see the inside of a jail. Some days I wished I could say the same.

My only detour was a brief stop for a couple of bottles of wine, my favorite nectar and Jean's as well. As I pulled in the driveway, Jorge greeted me. He was very talky, like most Siamese. He wanted even more attention than usual; maybe he could sense I was going to leave him alone. I checked the mail, listened to my messages, and watered a dozen orchids that I was fond of. I called Jean and told her that I would be by in about thirty minutes. Then I packed light for the weekend. I filled the automatic cat feeder, set the alarm, and I left.

Jean lived in a wonderful old neighborhood and had a precious bungalow her psychiatrist father had left her. She had really put her intelligence, education, and sense of humor to good use; he would be proud of her if he could see her today. I drove onto her driveway and tooted the horn. I didn't expect her to come running out. In fact, I knew that she wouldn't even be packed. As I approached the front door, she opened it and squealed, "I'm ready to rock and roll!"

"Surely you're not packed?"

"Hell, no. You know I wait until the last minute to do everything. There are so many interesting things to distract me along the way. Come help me—and by the way, I need to stop at the mall and buy some comfortable tennis shoes before we leave."

"It sounds like Las Vegas revisited."

"What do you mean?"

"We had to wash your clothes at midnight and then buy you sandals and pajamas the following morning. Then you insisted that we stop for seafood before we went to the airport."

She laughed. "We needed an ocean fix before going to the desert. We made it, didn't we?"

"No thanks to you."

"Let's be nice. This is the recipe for a good weekend: no work, good company, and no assholes to put up with."

"I'm ready for some R&R these days since I don't get much I&I," I said.

"What's I&I?"

"Intercourse and intoxication!"

"What have you done with Les and Michael? Is there something going on that I don't know about?"

"Nope, you know all my secrets."

I let it go at that. Jean was well aware that I had struggled in poverty while in law school from 1987 until 1990, met Les in 1993, married him a year later and had Michael immediately. I stayed home a lot with Michael for the first year, breast-feeding, loving, and nurturing him. I tried to do it by the book, the best I could, the best anybody could.

When the three of us moved back to Liberty, creating a new

client base meant long hours and hard work. I had been in practice for ten years, but a new law practice took at least two to three years to turn a good profit. Michael was five now, and Les had volunteered to take Michael with him to Denver for three months. It was his way of giving something back to me after I had sacrificed for the two of them.

In the end Les convinced me that it was best for all of us. He would have more time to spend with Michael than I did right now. For weeks I agonized about the separation. Finally, I relented. It was an opportunity for Les and Michael to bond, and let me concentrate on building another law practice.

"I'm almost packed. Did you bring the wine?"

"Two bottles—one for me and one for you. Funny how we worry about booze."

"Honey, I'm bringing four bottles. Can you imagine a town that doesn't sell beer or wine? What the hell do they do for entertainment?"

"I think they have different games and contests. You know, pin the tail on the school teacher, spin the rifle, shot-gun wedding day, and incest outcry day."

"You're right. The antique fair could be in a better town."

"We'll have a good time anyway. Good company, vino, old artifacts to look at, and no phones or faxes."

"Let's get the heck out of here. I'm surprised that the phone hasn't rung in the past fifteen minutes. If it does, let the recorder catch it—and don't forget my tennis shoes."

"You wouldn't let me." I rolled my eyes.

The drive was pleasant, and we talked nonstop, as always. We hadn't been away together in years.

"Micki, why did you go to that snakey swamp with Roy?"

"I didn't realize that it would be like that—and it was really beautiful out at the house. I'm glad I got to see it."

"Are you going back?"

"Probably not. Bob won't allow it."

"Does he still hold a grudge?"

"I'm afraid so. Not to change the subject, but that dream I had about you is still bothering me."

"Most dreams—good or bad—don't actually come true. Why

are you obsessing about it?"

"I get the feeling that it was a warning, but to who? You? Me?"

"I doubt it. It was probably just an imagination fart. I'd blame it on Roy, but you had the dream."

"It wasn't that bad. I loved being with Anna—and I even enjoyed looking at forensic evidence again."

"I never understood your fascination for all that weird shit."

"Speaking of weird, how is Guy?"

"Pretty good, but he asks me what to do about the shit in his crazy family—and then keeps on wallowing. I get tired of it."

"That's why I'm considering not taking any more divorce cases. They depress the hell out of me. Lately every divorce client has been a lunatic, a deviant, or a doormat. Years ago, it was easier for me to listen to their sad stories, but I can't do it anymore. I even cringe when my own family asks for help or advice. The stories get more and more bizarre. It makes me wonder how much of the population is normal."

I sighed, and Jean tried to comfort me. "Not many, we both know that. Our jobs make us work with lunatics."

I looked at the speedometer and increased my speed about ten miles an hour, then twenty, then thirty. Jean hollered, "Hey, what's the deal?"

"Someone is following us. Did you tell anyone where we were going?"

"Just my sister. It's Roy's fault you're feeling paranoid."

"No, I'm not. When I speed up, so do they. Pretty crappy tail, if you ask me. Let's find out for sure if they're following us."

I hit my brakes, went into a spin, and made a one-hundred-eighty-degree turn in the middle of the highway. The driver following me hit the brakes to avoid a collision. Smoke came from the tires, and the car appeared to sit still for a few seconds.

"Uh-oh. Here it comes again, right behind us. Shit!"

"I'm scared. With all your wild talk about bad dreams and dead bodies, what's all this about?"

"I don't know, but we're going to find out, if that car gets any closer. Look in my purse and hand me my gun. Now!"

"What are you going to do?"

"It depends on them."

A nondescript black sedan turned around and headed our direction.

I looked in the rearview mirror. It was accelerating fast. I saw a dirt road just ahead on the right. I jerked the car off the main road just in time.

Jean freaked out. "What if this is a dead end? What if it's a rapist or a killer? We wouldn't want our stalker to be distracted by potential rescuers or witnesses." Her voice became shrill.

"There's no need to be sarcastic."

I followed the road a few hundred yards and pulled over by a dilapidated fishing cabin. I got out of the car, .38 caliber snub-nosed revolver in hand, and ordered Jean to stay down no matter what.

The sedan also turned off. It moved slowly down the dirt road, and when it got close, I steadied my hand on the hood and fired twice—once at the passenger's window and again at the back windshield. Glass shattered after both shots. No one was sitting in the passenger seat, and I couldn't see the driver. This seemed to get their attention.

The car did a doughnut, spinning dirt and dust everywhere. They were nowhere in sight as I climbed back into the car. Jean was on the floorboard and refused to get up. I started the engine and pulled onto the highway. I let her stay on the floor for a few minutes longer, then asked, "Do you want to go on to Shelby, or would you like to go home?"

Jean was pissed.

No answer. I drove for about fifteen minutes. Finally she climbed back into her seat and asked, "Where are you headed?"

"To Shelby, unless you tell me otherwise."

"Let's go for it—unless you think it's dangerous." She warmed up to me again as her fear subsided.

"Whoever that was is long gone—for the time being."

"Micki, who would be following you?"

"What makes you think that they're following me?"

"You're the Quincy type."

"Maybe so, but they could have followed us from your house. Is something new going on with any of your crazy clients?"

"Not that I know of. I think it has something to do with that creepy case yesterday. This is all Roy's fault. He doesn't know squat. After all, he blew it with you over a mousy lab tech. Why the hell did you shoot at them?"

"I sure as hell wasn't going to wait for them to shoot at us. I aimed at the back window, but you wouldn't know that since you were on the floorboard."

"Damn straight."

"It's a good thing you listen to me once in a while."

"I'll be all right once we get to Shelby and I drink about two bottles of wine. I'll forget that any of this ever happened."

"In case this is my fault, I'm sorry I scared you."

"I'll get over being scared. I won't get over it if someone hurts you. That would really piss me off. When you get back to town, check into this. Okay?"

It was beginning to get dark. A neon sign on the front of a tiny grocery store and gas station looked pretty inviting. Jean and I agreed that a pee stop was in order after the big chase. When I was done, Jean entered the stall. I was washing my hands when I heard a loud crash. White porcelain shards lay all over the floor.

"What was that?" I asked.

Jean was laughing so hard she could barely talk. "I broke the toilet!"

"What?" By now I'm cracking up too.

"My purse strap caught on the lid and yanked it off. Should I tell the owner and offer to pay for it?"

"I guess so, but it's so embarrassing."

We composed ourselves and approached the attendant to pay for the damage. Once we got in the car, we laughed our asses off all the way to Shelby.

At last we saw a lighted porch and a welcome sign that proclaimed St. Elmo's Bed and Breakfast. As we got out, a frail, older woman peeked through the Venetian blinds. She opened the door slightly, and asked us if we were Miss Michelle and Miss Jean.

"Yes, ma'am. May we come in?" I asked.

She hesitated, then opened the door fully. She led us through a formal dining room filled with Victorian antiques, told us fresh-baked apple pie was waiting for us in the kitchen, and showed us our room. It was wonderful in every way, from the rich draperies to the turn-of-the-century counterpanes and the fresh spring flowers atop a hand-carved étagère. Instead of a closet, there was a large wardrobe. The room was filled with sterling silver candlesticks, marble-top tables, and interesting dresser pieces. I was in heaven. Jean came back from the bathroom carrying lots of tiny soaps and perfumes.

"Aren't they great?" she marveled.

"It's all great. Uncork some wine, my dear."

"Let's order a pizza," she coaxed.

Food comforted Jean; that's why she struggled with her weight. I was more concerned about mapping out an itinerary for tomorrow.

Since I had attended this show several times before, I knew exactly where to go. Most of the exhibitors preferred to hold their designated location year after year, hoping that previous customers would return and buy from them. I firmly believed that this strategy worked, as I was one of the return patrons. Jean lay back, yawned, and pulled the counterpane up over her head. She was more concerned with being able to sleep as late as possible.

"Are you sleepy?" I asked.

"Yes, I don't know why. Maybe it has something to do with seeing my life flash before my eyes."

"You're just coming down off an adrenalin high."

"You're probably right. Let's turn off the lights. It's after midnight."

"I'll wake you in the morning. Goodnight."

"Goodnight."

I was glad that Jean was sleepy, but I didn't think that I would sleep much tonight or any night in the near future. Not until I made some calls on Monday to Anna and Roy to see if they knew what the hell was going on. Maybe someone thought I was involved with the FBI or the local authorities.

What else could it be? Life had been rather calm since I married Leslie and had Michael—not boring, just steady and predictable. It's what I'd needed for years, and I'd never been happier. Until lately, I'd felt good about my life. Some unknown entity was threatening to snatch away my sense of security. I didn't like it, and I wasn't going to tolerate it. I lay awake for hours, and finally the sun peeked through the drapes.

I felt dull and lifeless. Maybe a shower would help. It was a little nippy out here in the piney woods. Jean hadn't stirred at all, and I didn't have the heart to wake her. Maybe she'd wake up when she smelled coffee brewing. I quickly showered, dressed, and made my way downstairs, where the aroma of frying bacon had permeated the air.

"Good morning, Michelle. How did you sleep?"

"Like a little lamb," I fibbed.

"Where's your friend? Jean, isn't it?"

"She's still sleeping."

"I'll keep breakfast warm for her. Does she want bacon, eggs, toast, and coffee?"

"She'd love that. Thank you for all your trouble."

"It's no trouble. Now sit down and we'll talk."

We ate and spoke of the cool, crisp weather, the sweet smells of spring, and the refreshing sounds of the birds chirping their songs. After I got directions to Shelby I got up and said I had to wake Jean so that we could get an early start.

I climbed the stairs and called out to the sleepyhead.

"Wake up, we need to get going. Don't want to miss out on all of the good deals.

"I know, I know. Give me another hour or so, or let me meet you there."

"That won't work. You don't have transportation, and it must be eight to ten miles to Shelby. Get your butt moving! I'll get your breakfast on a tray. It will be here when you get out of the shower."

"Have you already eaten?"

"Yes, I was up early. I didn't sleep very well."

"The shooting?"

"Let's not discuss it and ruin our day."

"You know I'm not a morning person. I must have my morning coffee before I move another muscle."

"All right. I'll get it and leave it in the bathroom for you."

I went back downstairs for Jean's coffee. Our hostess was

nowhere in sight, so I poured the coffee myself and found a tray to carry Jean's breakfast upstairs. I couldn't wait until Sunday to call Anna about what happened yesterday. I looked around for a phone. I didn't see one anywhere. Could it be that Helen didn't have a phone? It was possible. All of my communication with her had been written.

I put Jean's breakfast in our room, then tiptoed into the bathroom and left her coffee. She was in the shower.

I ran down the stairs. I had to get into town and call Anna before Jean got dressed and wondered where I was. I remembered seeing a pay phone outside the store where we stopped last night. I drove like a maniac, and it took me about one minute to get there. I grabbed my calling card and dialed Anna's number.

"Hi, it's me. I'm sorry to call so early, but this can't wait."

"I thought you were out of town?"

"I am. Listen, someone followed me here, or tried to anyway. I noticed them a couple of hours outside of town. I mean, I wasn't paying attention or I might have spotted them sooner."

"Who was it?"

"I don't know. That why I'm calling you. I shot at the stalker's car. I guess I'm lucky they didn't shoot back. I think this has something to do with the case you're working. Has anything weird happened to you since Thursday?"

"No, but I've been at the lab most of the time working on a backlog of cases. I have to get caught up before this mystery case takes on hurricane force. It looks as if it's already at the tropical storm stage, from what you're telling me. What do you want me to do?"

"Call Roy, and have him call anyone at the department he can trust. He'll know where to sniff."

"What else?"

"I'll call you back tonight.

"Call me back around eight, and be careful," she warned. "Maybe you should come home?"

"No, I think I'm pretty safe out here in the woods. It's so-called civilization that scares me."

It was back to the races as I headed to the B&B before Jean emerged from the bathroom. I didn't want to alarm her. Although

I'd kill her if she went back to sleep. Maybe not kill her, but I'd at least use ice water in her face. I skidded into the oyster shell driveway and jumped from the driver's seat. As I climbed the staircase, Jean looked over the balcony and asked me where I'd been.

"Just out to the car to load up a few things we may need today."

She seemed satisfied."I hope you appreciate the fact that I'm losing my beauty sleep to hunt treasures with you."

"I do, I do."

"Let's get going before I need another cup of coffee. Can we have the sun roof open?"

"Absolutely. Got your wish list?"

"Yes, but I don't think I need it," Jean said happily.

We drove the scenic highway to Shelby. The pine smell permeated the air, and I took deep, deep breaths. I felt better by the time we reached our first stop. There were already hundreds of cars parked, and even more people. It was refreshing not to see a single soul I knew.

We walked around all morning and noted items that we were interested in. We got the best cash price from the dealer and moved on. A couple of hours later we'd circle back to buy the things we couldn't live without. I was leaning toward a black forest jewelry box with birds carved on top, and a lovely alabaster bust of a woman wearing a hat. Jean found a pair of open barley twist candlesticks, some fruit prints, and several items of sterling silver .

After lunch we forged ahead in search of more treasures. We spent all afternoon walking from tent to tent, booth to booth, bending over to examine collectible pieces of everything imaginable. At the end of the day, we lucked out because what we wanted was still available. About six o'clock, we were sunburned and exhausted, so we departed for the bed and breakfast. The car was about a mile from where we ended up, and we started the long walk back.

We stopped at a small market and bought chicken salad, french bread, fruit, and gourmet cookies. My car eased into Helen's driveway, and I killed the engine. We walked wearily to the front door and knocked.

Helen let us in and said, "The door is always open. Just come on in."

Jean headed upstairs, and I called after her, "You shower first. I need to run up to the convenience store since we aren't going out tonight."

"We just got back from the store."

"I know, but I left my digital phone at home, and I need to call Leslie from the payphone."

"Are you going to tell him about the incident?"

"I don't know. He's so far away, and there's nothing he can do from Colorado."

"I'll be out by the time you get back. I'll fix supper, since you got breakfast for me."

What the hell was I thinking, or not thinking, to leave my beloved digital phone at home? I called Leslie first. He answered on the second ring, and I could hear Michael in the background.

"Hi, babe. How are you and Michael?"

"Pretty good, but we miss you."

"Me too. How about if I come up next Wednesday evening and stay through the weekend?"

"Great. You want to talk to Michael?"

It was good to hear his little voice. Then I told Les I'd take the seven o'clock flight.

After that I called Anna. She didn't answer the damn phone, so I left her a message. "Anna, it's me. I was calling to see if you found out anything yet. I'll call you tomorrow night when I get home."

I felt frustrated and paranoid, as are most people who have a great deal of exposure to law enforcement. Now I had to wait and see, which meant another sleepless night, waiting and wondering. Head down, I walked in slow motion toward the car. My head jerked upward just in time to catch a glimpse of a dark-colored sedan speeding up the highway. They didn't see me, because I'd parked around the back of the store. Being more paranoid seemed in order.

The sons-of-bitches were still trying to follow me. Someone knows we're here. I waited a few minutes to see if the car returned, and when it didn't, I left the store and drove back to Jean. She had a nice picnic dinner on the floor, with wine and all the fixings. She seemed relaxed, and I didn't want to worry her.

"Make your calls?" she asked.

"Everyone is fine. I decided to fly up and see Leslie and Michael next weekend in Denver. That's really going to complicate my week. With only three work days, I don't know how I'll get it all done before Thursday."

"You'll manage. Let's eat. I'm starved."

"Me too. Who would have guessed that antiquing can be such hard work?"

"I'm lucky to have a friend blessed with good taste who knows a good find from a piece of junk."

"Thanks," I said and smiled. I love being appreciated.

We ate chicken salad sandwiches, lots of fruit, and drank wine. I excused myself and went to shower. When I returned, Jean was in bed reading a Truman Capote novel. I flipped through an *Architectural Digest*; I was planning to redecorate the house. Next I read my bar journal. Then I tried to finish a murder mystery I began a month or so ago. How appropriate.

"Ready for me to turn out the lights?" Jean asked after a couple of hours.

"I just hope I can sleep."

"One last thing before lights out. I was thinking maybe we should go back a different route."

"Don't worry about it. I think we lost them."

Another restless night with dark images and strange dreams left me less than perky the next morning, but we packed the car and left early for our last treasure hunt.

I bought Leslie another miner's lamp. Now he has twenty. For Michael, I started a collection of old toys, mainly trains.

The drive home was uneventful, but the conversation was engaging as always. "Remember the night we made sand tarts for Christmas?" Jean asked.

"To this day, I don't know what we did wrong—other than drink too much wine before baking them."

"Maybe we can try again this Christmas. We're better cooks now." Jean was always an optimist.

"I never claimed to be a good cook. I get by though."

"Well, just because we aren't Martha Stewart doesn't mean we don't have other talents. We're both educated, intelligent, employed, and funny."

"And we're modest, too!" I added.

Then we were quiet for the last few minutes of our drive home. Jean broke the silence.

"I already have the Monday blahs. I mean, why do we have to work? It interferes with everything that I want to do, like write or read or lie on the beach."

"You probably won't work forever. You do have a nest egg that will keep you comfortable, but us poor folk must keep on keeping on."

"I'm afraid not to work. I may run out of money and where would I be then? I'd be the oldest blonde in the world without a dime for a bottle of hair color."

You won't run out of money unless you try. And what a description of yourself—really, be honest."

"I am being honest. Promise me if I die you'll make sure my roots are done."

"You're being silly. Here we are, home at last." I sighed as we drove up to Jean's house. I was already feeling eerie without her talking about dying.

"Call me when you get back from Denver next weekend. I'm here if you need me."

"Let me help you with your bags, we wouldn't want to break anything." I avoided her eyes.

I carried her bags and purchases as far as the front porch, made my excuses for not staying, and then walked slowly back to the car.

Chapter Ten

*D*riving home, I wondered if there would be a message from Anna on my machine. I engaged the garage door opener and entered. Jorge leapt in to greet me. "How's my kitty cat today?" I scratched his head and ears. Jorge meowed again and again.

I walked in the back door to my house and checked the recorder. No calls. What a wonder. After I carried my things inside, I paged Anna. This couldn't wait a moment longer. While I was unpacking, Anna called me back.

"Micki girl, is that you?"

"It's me all right. Have you found out anything?"

"Oh, yeah. I'm calling on my mobile phone from the bayou. We've been out here all weekend. Why don't you come on out, and I'll fill you in."

"Is Bob there?"

"We haven't been able to reach him."

"That place is so far out in the swamp. I don't know if I could find it again."

"I'll send one of the guys out to the main road. What time would you want them to pick you up on the highway?"

"Maybe about five o'clock. I really should stay home and get some work done before tomorrow morning, but I'm more interested in what's going on out there. I'll meet whoever you send out at highway marker 229. I ran out of gas there one time, so I know where it is."

"And make certain that no one is following you."

"Should there be?"

"I won't say anymore over the phone." Anna hung up.

I changed into jeans and a denim shirt, grabbed my digital phone and some food for us, should this turn into an all-nighter, then hopped back into my car. I'd have to gas up again. Damn, I was beginning to live in my car. After leaving the gas station, I circled the downtown area to see if I had picked up another tail. As far as I could see, no one was interested in me today.

I decided to call Leslie and tell him that I got home safely from Shelby so he wouldn't worry if I didn't call tonight. Hell, I didn't know how long I'd be out there, but I wasn't leaving that mansion without some answers. No answer in Denver, so I left him a message: "Les, I got back about an hour ago, and I'm on my way to a crime scene to help Anna. If it's late when I get home, then I'll call you in the morning. Love you and Michael."

He's not the worrying kind, but I hadn't told him the whole story. I didn't know the whole story, and until I got the big picture, there would be no discussion of any of this with anyone but Anna or Roy. I usually accused Les of not sharing information with me, but this time it was me holding back.

"Over here, doll." Roy was grinning. "I have the pleasure of your company again, and such a short time has passed."

"She sent you, huh?"

"Who else? Anna knows how I feel about you, so she did me a favor."

"Why she likes you is a mystery to me."

"Because I'm so good-looking and charming."

"If you say so. I always thought modesty was your best quality."

"Micki, let me hide your car in the trees like we did before. We don't need any unwanted company."

"Are you going to fill me in on what's going on?"

"Well, we've found some pretty amazing stuff in the house and barn. Some of it's kind of eerie. Anna will want to show you everything. Not to change the subject, but I've been thinking about you. Will you have lunch with me next week?"

"Why?"

"To catch up and talk about old times."

"I'm happy now, and I don't want to remember those old times."

"Then we won't reminisce. We'll just catch up on what's been happening in both of our lives lately."

"Somehow, it doesn't sound like a good idea."

"No strings attached. I'll behave myself."

"Sure you will," I replied.

This boat ride was just as creepy as the first one. We didn't talk much. I must have hurt his feelings by being noncommittal about lunch. He didn't take rejection or criticism very well. Any better than I took betrayal and embarrassment.

We anchored alongside the other police boats, unmarked of course. Four boats were docked side by side. Anna came running out of the house.

"Come see what we've found. How strong is your stomach today?"

"Is it that bad?"

"It's pretty grim. Let's start outside the house near the barn."

We walked along a paved brick path and came to a big hole that had just been excavated. There was a large concrete container next to it. Anna pointed to a body bag lying alongside.

"What's that?" I asked.

"Haven't you ever seen a septic tank?"

"I guess I haven't," I responded. "I've always lived in the city with all the amenities. Who's in the body bag?"

"We don't know yet. We can't even estimate how long it's been in the septic tank."

"What horror of a human being could do this to another?" I wondered out loud.

"Maybe the victim deserved it," Anna offered.

"Could be, but my best guess is a Jeffrey Dahmer, a Charles Manson, or a Wayne Williams did it. Taking the pessimistic view, I know how intelligent evil can be. I'm saying murder. Was there trauma to the body?"

"I found a bullet hole in the skull," Anna replied.

"Male or female?"

"I'm guessing male, but I'm no pathologist. We'll know by tomorrow. Hopefully the FBI can make a positive identification of the John or Jane Doe by the end of the week."

"Have you found any other dead bodies out here?"

"Not yet, but come see what else we've discovered."

I followed Anna into the house. We climbed the staircase leading into the attic.

In this part of the country people always hid stuff in their attics. Because houses were below sea level, they didn't have basements. I saw several old antique trunks. Anna bent forward and opened one, so I could look inside. On top there were lots of packages of coffee. Underneath the coffee were bound papers.

Anna quizzed me, "What kind of legal documents are these?"

I eased one volume from the trunk to examine it. "This is a transcript. Anna, it's Wayne's transcript. Remember, I worked the crime scene," I say excitedly. "I never did understand why it was a mistrial. I mean, the evidence was overwhelming. I wasn't an attorney at the time, so I didn't have the right to question the District Attorney's office."

"This is getting close to home, Micki. Now, it makes sense that we're drawn into this investigation."

"What do you mean 'we'? Do you think this involves me too? I've been away a long time."

"Well, you were working at the lab when Wayne was murdered. You investigated it, and no one seems opposed to your being here. So yes, I do."

"Why won't anyone talk about this?" I felt exasperated.

"It's up to us to figure that out." Anna was emphatic.

"The FBI is a mute organization at this point," she added.

"God, how I hate them. They're oppressive, abusive, prejudiced, and just plain stupid."

Anna interrupted my ranting. "Don't get yourself worked up, girl. We better think clearly now and get us a plan to solve this mystery on our own. We've got us a whole new nightmare."

I calmed down and suggested to Anna that she hide the transcripts at the lab. For the time being they'd be our secret. Then she led me outside.

"I didn't find anything else of interest up here, so let's move to the water well outside."

"What did you find out there?"

"A nine millimeter, a set of keys, and a pair of surgical gloves."

Everyone else was searching a two-hundred-yard perimeter around the house. Ever since Roy dodged a bullet, he wanted to be sure no one was lurking around with a silencer.

"Here they are!" Anna exclaimed.

"How did you find this stuff?" I asked.

"I pointed my flashlight down the well, and the bricks looked different right about here. I dug around with a screw driver. One of the bricks was loose. I took it out, and then another, and another. They were inside a leather pouch."

"Have you told anyone yet?" I asked.

"Not yet. They've all been busy looking for other bodies."

"Hold off telling them till we finish today. Let's give ourselves a chance to put some pieces together."

Anna agreed.

"What else do you have that they haven't seen yet?"

"Some ledgers, books, cash—that kind of thing."

"Where are they?"

"In the armoire in the master bedroom."

"Let's have a look. By the way, why isn't Bob here?"

"I don't know. He must be binging bad these days."

"I think he's staying away on purpose. If he missed day one of a crime scene, particularly one with a potentially high profile, he'd never miss after that." I was certain. He was typical of weak people with power and rank.

"That's true, but he hasn't been himself in a long time, Micki. He's made great strides in his quest to hit rock bottom. Something in his life changed when you were gone, and I don't mean his rocky marriage. Something's eating him alive, and I can't figure it out. In all the years that I've worked for him, he's never said much about himself. There's a good possibility I wouldn't want to know the truth. Know what I mean?"

"If you knew his secrets, it could make you feel responsible and accountable to others."

The master bedroom was a lovely room. It belonged to someone who cared about it very much. It was hard to imagine such
grandeur as the site of a crime.

"Where did you find the money and paperwork?"

"Behind that picture of water lilies, in a wall safe. I removed
everything."

"How did you get it open?"

"It wasn't locked. All I did was look behind all the pictures.

"That's pretty weird. Why would anyone bother to use a wall
safe, and then leave it unlocked? Maybe the guy in the septic tank
opened the safe and someone killed him before he could relock
it."

No comment from Anna was forthcoming. She was concen-
trating elsewhere.

"I didn't find any floor safe in here, but let's check the closet,"
Anna suggested.

There was no floor safe in the closet, either.

We catalogued the ledgers, books, and cash—a lot of cash. It
was so much money that we didn't have time to count it all. We
examined the ledgers, but were unable to make anything of them.
We weren't certain what priority to give these items. They didn't
tie into the case yet.

Anna looked up at me. "What is it?" I asked.

"Do you ever think of doing forensic work again?"

"Not really. I don't miss the bureaucratic barbed wire. Once
you're a lawyer, it's who you are. You think differently and react
differently. You don't fit in anymore, except with other lawyers.
Even my family thinks I'm weird."

"I don't think you're weird."

"But you work in law enforcement, and you understand the
attraction. Besides, you know both sides of my personality."

"What do you like about being a lawyer? I know you don't
like the public image."

"My practice is an amalgamation of my preferences, profi-
ciencies, and profit. I take cases that I like, or ones that interest
me. I take those that I know I'm good at, and I do it to make
money. It hasn't always been that way. In the beginning I took
whatever came to the door, but I feel more in control of my life

and my livelihood. That's what I like—even if it is a fantasy."

"It hasn't been the same without you. It's lonely, and I don't get much support at the lab. I end up on crime scenes alone a lot of the time." Anna exhaled slowly.

"Maybe you should encourage Bob to hire someone dependable and trainable," I suggested.

"Trainable being the important attribute," Anna admitted. "Lately, all of our prospects need constant supervision. In this field you have to be able to work alone as well as cooperatively."

"Anna, if you need me to, I'll see this one through with you. Don't think that I'm being overly charitable. The case genuinely interests me."

"Thanks. Do you think we should tell the guys about the gun and paperwork I found?"

"I guess so. I wouldn't want to be charged with interfering with an investigation. Let the sergeant look it over before you carry it back to the lab tonight. How many rooms are left to search?"

"Several. This case is taking a lot of time, and I'm getting further and further behind at the lab. All I can do right now is gather evidence. There's no time to actually test anything. We got in a new DNA thermal cycler and genetic analyzer that I haven't even unpacked yet. We're beginning to solve old cases with mitochondrial DNA and CODIS, which stands for combined DNA index system. Several unsolved cases involving pedophiles have been cleared due to hits on CODIS. I'd like to continue working the cases concerning re-offenders, but this case is shoving everything to the back burner. Our ambitious DA is going to have a hissy fit when he finds out how far behind the lab is. I get depressed just talking about it."

"Just send him a sample bottle of perfume from the septic tank. Maybe that'll remind him that you're overworked and underpaid—like most county employees. Hell, you need help, and lots of it. Maybe this case will be the ticket. Get far enough behind and they'll hire you some help."

"If I send him a sample of the funk I found this morning, he'll surely come screaming. That shit is stronger than stud horse piss with the foam farted off."

I laughed. Anna had the funniest, folksiest, oddest sayings I'd ever heard. Said she got them from her mother.

"Send it to him anyway," I said. "It'll be good for the DA to get a taste—or smell—of what you put up with on a daily basis."

"Yeah, those prosecutors live in a bubble, insulated from all the gore. The most they have to endure is some grizzly photos. Let them make a crime scene early one Sunday morning instead of going to church. Have the DA's office remove evidence from the battered body of a rape victim or the victim of a hit and run—or even worse a murdered individual whose brains are splattered all over the floor. Let them see it, smell it, grieve over it, gather it, analyze it, report it, testify to it—and ultimately be harassed in court by some defense attorney. The worst part is when they screw up, and it ends in a mistrial. Or even worse, the case is reversed on appeal." Her speech stirred grim memories for both of us. I hoped she didn't see me as a harassing defense attorney.

"You mean like Wayne's case?" I had to ask.

"It still tears me up that Jake Edmonds is still walking around out there. The state seems to have no intention of retrying the SOB. The damn DA cares more about fund-raising for his rise to the legislature. Greedy bastard."

"I think it's possible that this case is tied to Wayne's demise. The transcripts from the murder trial are here in this house, a house that the FBI insists on having searched inch by inch. We're just trace evidence away from making a determination as to what it is that the feds are looking for. Get to work on the forensics, and I think you'll soon get some direction. I'll stay in touch and help as much as I can."

When Anna revealed her findings to Pagden, he wasn't very impressed. Compared to the body, they were anticlimactic.

I stood beside her for a few minutes to determine if there was anything unusual going on in the law enforcement sector. They had been uncharacteristically quiet during this investigation. I wondered who silenced them. My guess was the feds.

"Anna, where's Roy?"

"I haven't seen him since you got here."

"There's a lot of legal work waiting for me at home. Next

week is going to be a bitch of a short week. Wednesday night I'm going to Denver to see Leslie and Michael."

"I'll help you look for Roy. And I promise not to bother you with any of this again until you get back."

Chapter Eleven

"*H*ey, you two. Over here," Roy shouted.

He called to us from behind the stables. He was bent down on one knee looking at something. We stood in a grove of magnolia trees that smelled so sweet it was almost sickening.

"What is it, Roy? And where the hell did you disappear to?" I was testy, to put it mildly.

"Well, the answer to your second question is, I've been right here, and the answer to your first question is, I don't know."

Anna and I leaned over to see what Roy had found. It appeared to be a map of some sort.

"Where did you find it?" Anna asked sweetly. She felt sorry for Roy because I wouldn't cut him any slack. Men are men to her; cheating is integral to their character.

"It was hanging way up there in a tree. It was folded up inside a workman's belt, you know the kind that you hang your tools from. I got one of the fishing rod and reels from the barn and hooked it. It took awhile to bring it down, and that's where I've been. I just this very moment found the map." He held the map up for us to see.

Anna grabbed the map, examined it, and said, "It looks like something is buried down at the beach off of old State Highway

87. That road has been closed for years. The state won't maintain it because of the frequent storms and hurricane damage. It won't be easy to reach by car."

"What makes you think this is a map of buried treasure?" I asked in a quiet voice.

"It's marked off in feet, and there's an X right here, so someone buried something out there. I'm sure of it. Let's go dig it up." Her eyes were shining. A chill went down my spine as our eyes met. "It looks like an all-nighter. You up to it?" Anna's voice was quivering with excitement.

"Are we going to ride all the way out there? I can't believe it."

"We have to. Our evidence up until now is just evidence. It doesn't give us any direction." Anna was emphatic.

"What a bad week this is going to be. This detour won't help me a bit."

Anna looked at Roy and grinned, "You coming with us?"

"Why not? Let me tell the sergeant we're off on a mission." He laughed.

"Just like old times, huh, Micki?" Anna nodded at me.

"Old times—the good, the bad, and the ugly. Right, Roy?" I gave him a look.

We gathered the evidence collected so far and walked toward the boats. Roy met us a few minutes later. I guess he had to get permission to leave. We made the now familiar boat ride back to our cars. It would be dark by the time we got back, so Anna and I agreed that it would be simpler to leave our cars in a park-and-ride lot near the main highway that led to our respective houses. Once our cars were deposited, Anna grabbed the crime scene kit and a large box of assorted forensic tools. Roy put everything in the back of his unmarked van.

It's not like we hadn't made crime scenes at the beach in years past, it had just been awhile. No one spoke for some time. Then Roy asked Anna, "Do you think that you could talk Micki into having lunch with me next week? Or dinner? I'll settle for either."

Anna looked sheepishly at me from the front seat, and I shook my head and mouthed, "No way." I hoped Roy wasn't looking at me in his rearview mirror.

She hesitated, and then made my excuses.

"Micki is a little short on time next week. She's leaving Wednesday night for Denver to see her family."

"How about the next week?" he asked.

Anna looked at me again, and again I shook my head, "No." I thought to myself, What a silly fucking game for a grown woman to play. I should speak for myself and let Anna off the hook.

"Roy, just call my office week after next, and I'll see if I can work you in."

"I don't need an appointment. I just want to have lunch with you."

"I adhere to a strict schedule—until recently, that is. It's the only way I can survive in my chosen profession, the one you think you love so much. So if you want to have lunch with me, you'll have to call and make an appointment."

"Love what so much, you or your profession?"

"I don't know, Roy. You tell me."

"I'll call, I'll call."

It got real quiet after that. Anna looked at Roy like he was pitiful or cute or both. Then she gave me a half smile like she was sorry that Roy was tempting me to pick up where we left off. I had never liked having serious conflicts in a car. Like when I was younger and some dude tried to corner me. I had to sit and take it, fight it out, let them kiss me, or try to have sex with me, lecture me, or tell me how crazy I was. Here I was, older and wiser, but still having the same bullshit confrontations I always had with men, and in a fucking car. I thought I had become immune to all this since I met Leslie. But it never goes away. How old must you be before the games subside? I had to get over a quick fix, a cheap thrill.

"Should be plenty of light tonight, it's a full moon." Anna couldn't stand tense silences.

It had been a rough ride on the eroded highway to the beach. "I hope we find what we're looking for." I said.

Roy eased off the highway onto the sandy beach road and asked Anna to read the directions.

"'Drive one mile south of the Sea Rim exit toward Emerald Beach, look for the tallow tree that is growing at a 45° angle, pace off twenty feet west of the tree, stop, and dig.' Pretty simple, I'm sure whoever hid it believed it wouldn't be discovered in that tree, or else they would have written the directions in code."

We drove one mile south and there it was: a gnarled old tallow tree. My brothers and I always called them chinaberry trees. Roy stopped the car, pulled a Lufkin tape measurer from his pocket, and faced us. Anna and I walked to the rear of the car to retrieve the well-worn crime scene kit. Roy marked off twenty feet, Anna handed him a small spade, and he began to dig.

Roy continued digging while Anna and I watched. After he had dug down about two feet, he stopped.

"Get me a shovel. This is obviously not a shallow grave." We had all assumed it was a grave.

I ran to the car to get a shovel, and handed it to Roy. He continued digging for a good fifteen minutes. The sand was coarse and heavy. It was not wet. Whoever buried the object of our search knew where the tide lines were. The area around the tree would never be covered by surf unless there was a bad tropical storm or a hurricane. Roy finally hit metal, kept digging, and unearthed a large black metal box. Anna and I leaned forward with our gloved hands outstretched and lifted the box from the sand. It was latched, but wasn't locked. We opened it to find a large brown envelope that contained a crime lab label (our crime lab label) on the outside. The label listed the contents of the envelope.

"What the hell is this doing here?" Anna looked at me with disbelieving eyes.

"What is it?"

"Evidence from Wayne's case. You're right, Micki. The two cases are linked. This wouldn't be buried here if something strange weren't going on. I assumed this evidence was still locked in the vault at work. After the mistrial, we had to store it for any future trials. Who the hell is trying to hide this stuff, and why?"

"I hate to bring this up since it hits so close to home, but Bob has a beach cabin right near here." I hesitated to say it, but I needed confirmation from the two of them. I knew that Anna was protective of the SOB.

"That's right," she said. "But, I can't imagine what his involvement could be." She opened the envelope and compared the contents to what was listed on the front submission label.

"One nine millimeter semi-automatic, one baggie containing several hairs, one baggie containing fibers, and one white blood-stained T-shirt."

"Is it all there?" I asked.

"I can't remember right now, but I think this is all that was submitted to the lab. You worked the case, Micki. What do you remember?"

"It's been so long."

"Well, please remember, because I wasn't there. I was out of town with my sweetie. You took dumb-ass Cindy with you to process Wayne's body and to the crime scene. What did you remove from the body?"

"Just took the usual photographs, the pathologist provided his clothes and his cowboy hat, and then I collected swabs for ballistics testing. I remember asking the pathologist where all of Wayne's rings were, but he didn't know. Later at the scene, I found out that Roy had his rings and his wallet full of money. I brought back hairs, fibers, prints, and photos from the crime scene and submitted them to the lab."

"Micki, you do know that Bob knew Wayne?"

"Yeah, I remember. Wayne used to come pick you up for lunch. After I met Wayne, he would pick us both up for lunch on his way to his broker's office. He loved to play the market."

"And the ponies," she added cheerfully.

"That was fun. He always called the bookies on the way to Delta Downs to get a list of the winners for each race of the evening. I never picked a winner in my life until we went to the races with Wayne. We could sit in the clubhouse, eat steak, drink a bottle or two of Mateus, and have a grand old time. Remember, Roy?" Roy had gone to a few races with me when we were dating.

"Uh, yeah," he stammered.

Anna and I both looked at Roy. He appeared to be in a trance. Until this moment, we hadn't realized that Roy had been completely mute since we opened up the box. He appeared to be in shock.

"Cat got your tongue, Roy?" I chided.

"No, I'm trying to figure out how and why this police evidence got buried at the beach."

"You mean crime lab evidence, don't you? After all, it remains with the lab until the time we receive a destruction order for it," Anna said.

"Whatever. Let's not argue about semantics," he said.

"Roy has learned some big words since I left town." I couldn't help teasing him.

He ignored my catty comment. I felt a little ashamed of myself, so I kept my mouth shut for awhile. Roy pulled me to the side while Anna was busy collecting the evidence we had just recovered.

He whispered in my ear, "I have to see you next week before you leave. It's important. Please."

"Why?"

"I need your professional help, Micki. You're the only one who I can trust with this. I'm serious. This is not some ploy to get your attention. My life and my livelihood are at stake. I'm ready to explain where you fit into all of this."

"Does this have something to do with the gun we just found?"

"Absolutely, and it involves Belle."

"Who's Belle?" I was impatient, but I kept my voice down.

"It's not a who, it's a what. The mansion out there in the bayou."

"So all of this is connected? I knew it." I slapped him on the shoulder.

"Yes, but I only know what Bob's told me, and I'm beginning to think maybe he didn't tell me the whole story. I don't want to say any more in front of Anna, because this thing goes deep. It involves the sheriff's office, the police department, and the crime lab. Will you meet me tomorrow afternoon? Not at your office — I don't want anyone to see me there."

"I'll meet you at the football stadium. We can sit there unnoticed. Seven o'clock tomorrow night all right with you?"

"Thank you, Micki."

"Sure."

"What are you two whispering about?" Anna asked.

"Not much," I fibbed. "Roy is still dreaming about the two of us having a nooner."

He grinned. "I wish. Maybe Anna can convince you."

Anna came to my rescue. "Give it up, Roy. She's happily married."

"Not as long as I'm alive. I think you both know that."

"You've carried a rather large torch, Roy, for more years than I care to count. It would give away my age." Anna chuckled to herself.

"It's more than a torch. Besides, I want Micki to forgive me for all the stunts I pulled."

"Like fucking my lab assistant while we were dating. You call that a stunt. I call it unforgivable." I still couldn't control my emotions.

"I wanted you, Micki. I just couldn't get you to care for me the way I cared for you."

"You should have given it time. I don't fall in love overnight."

"But you were so hung up on that married guy. I felt like I was just mild entertainment for you."

"That was your interpretation, Roy. I never felt that way. Your ego couldn't wait long enough for me to recover from a crappy, long-term relationship."

"I guess timing is everything." Roy pouted.

"Maybe, but mostly it's about understanding, commitment, and trust—none of which you ever demonstrated to me."

"I would have done anything for you."

"Anything that involved fucking me around. Isn't that all you really wanted?

"Why don't you admit it was only physical attraction on your part? Let's just do it right here in the sand and be done with it. Then you can get on with your life. You'll have one more notch in your belt, and one less wet dream. No pun intended.

"You can tell all the guys at the department about your wet sex on the beach. How about it?" Roy looked like a whipped pup.

Anna had walked away when I started losing it. I was trying to confront Roy's flirtation and claim control for myself. Years ago there had been a few select men, those who touched me emotionally and passionately, and during those relationships, I lost all self-control. I did impulsive, erotic things that felt good, exciting, and sexy. They made every inch of my body feel alive, and I let my imagination run free. I've had sex every place imaginable, on the hoods and trunks of cars, in showers and swimming pools, elevators, no-tell motels, you name it. Doing it on the floor of my office was a favorite. Why was there sexual tension here?

I never had sex with Roy. Maybe I resented him screwing it up. I wasn't ready then, and he had been too ready. I couldn't feel like this. It wasn't appropriate now, but the air was charged with electricity, and I knew that I was losing control again. After all of those years with unresolved feelings for Roy, the time had come to face the issues between us. He was going to complicate our relationship even further after our meeting tomorrow.

"Let's go," Anna shouted from the car.

We drove back in silence. I had humiliated Roy, and I was suddenly exhausted from the previous sleepless nights and the long drive from Shelby. We entered the parking lot, and Anna got out. She opened the trunk and loaded her car with crime scene gear and evidence from the beach. I ran around to help her, but she was already getting in the driver's seat by the time I removed myself and my belongings from Roy's van.

"Let's have dinner Tuesday night, Anna," I suggested.

"Sounds good. And you better resolve things with Roy before Leslie comes home."

"There's nothing to resolve."

"Don't kid yourself. It's so strong I can smell it."

"I thought I was all grown up and finished with him, Anna."

"He never completely went away, Micki, but that's a good fantasy you got going for yourself."

"That's not a comforting thought, but probably true." I drew a deep breath. "Shit, now I'm alone with Roy. He's waiting for me."

"Just tell him bye and go home."

I walked over to Roy's van. He looked up at me. I got really uncomfortable with what I was feeling. Maybe I was just lonely or bored, but it seemed more than that.

"Will you see me tomorrow?"

"Professionally, right?"

"Right."

"I'll be there. If I'm a little late, wait for me. Tomorrow is a full day."

"I will." He stepped from his van, took my hand, and put it to his cheek. He pulled me close to him, pressed himself hard against my body, and then released me abruptly.

I stood there for a moment looking at him, because I couldn't move. A wave of something powerful ran through my body. I looked away for a moment, and then I left. As I drove home, I felt relieved to be away from the bayou, the beach, and Anna and Roy. They reminded me of the past, a past where I had less of everything, including resolve. "It's so strong I can smell it." God, she was right. Crude, but right.

Chapter Twelve

*H*ome again, finally. I felt as if I had been away for weeks. The weekend in Shelby had been enjoyable, but with two trips to the swamp and a drive to the beach, it had all been too much for me.

"Hello, Jorge, have you been lonely?" He meowed back in response to my one-sided conversation. Since Les left for Denver, Jorge had been my sole companion. That reminded me that I had promised to call Les tonight when I got home. What time was it? Twelve. It was getting late. The phone rang. It was Les.

"Hi, babe. I got your message. How was your trip home?"

"Uneventful, but relaxing. How's Michael?"

"He's fine, having a great time up here."

"Les, I was called out to that crime scene again today. Then we made a trip out to the beach. We found a dead body in the septic tank at the swamp house and some incriminating evidence at the beach. It looks like this case is linked to a murder case that was tried years ago, when I worked at the lab."

"Why are you involved?" He always hated anything that did-n't include him.

"I've been asking myself the same question. Anna asked for my help again today and I said I would. Besides I have a lot of unanswered questions. Les, someone followed me and Jean to Shelby this weekend."

"How do you know that?"

"Well, it was pretty obvious after awhile. They had followed me for some time before it registered. When I suspected that we were being followed, I spun around in the middle of the highway, and they did the same. I fired off a few shots at their car."

"What!"

"It sounds bad, but it wasn't really. Although Jean was white as a ghost for awhile. I pulled off the road, and when the stalker turned off in pursuit, I had Jean get down in the floor and I fired at them. Just to scare them away from us."

"Did it work?"

"I think so."

"I don't like this, Micki. I can't protect you if something happens again."

"I'm okay. Don't worry. I didn't want to tell you about it, but I didn't want to hide it either."

"I don't know what to do for you." He never did.

"You don't have to do anything. Just pick me up at the airport Wednesday night."

"I'll be there, and if anything else threatens your welfare, I want to hear about it. All right."

"All right. I have some legal work to catch up on, so I'll say goodnight now."

"Goodnight. Take care of yourself." His voice was tender.

I reviewed a few files and read some offense reports in preparation for Monday's clients. I went to bed at one. Lately my sleep had been disturbed with strange, restless dreams. In the courtroom dreams I was a chemist-toxicologist, testifying in a murder trial. In the bedroom scenes, I wasn't with Les. The face of my lover was blurred.

When I awoke, I felt hung over. The worst part about the dream hangover was the guilt. That old Catholic guilt had been ingrained in my soul since birth and still pervaded my conscience. I was so preoccupied that I thought less and less about my clients and their cases. But the worst part of the guilt was my unresolved feelings for Roy. I wanted to be rid of those feelings, and I was willing to do whatever it took to resolve the situation, once and for all.

I woke up listening to Billy Joel singing "Big Shot." I got ready in a fog. When I got to work, Sherry greeted me with a cheery "How was your weekend?"

"Strange. I'm making crime scenes again with my old lab partner. I swore I'd never look at another dead body, but never say never."

"Pretty bad weekend then, huh?"

"Not all bad. Shelby was fun. If you have any unusual phone calls, hang-ups, anything out of the ordinary—let me know. This case I'm working on involves more than a suspect and a victim. As a matter of fact, keep an eye out for any weird things happening around the office."

"Weirder than our regular clientele?"

"You'll know. This is different."

"Well, you're all clear this morning. No one is screaming in my ear yet, and you don't have any court appearances until tomorrow. Consider it an uneventful Monday—except for the calendar being double booked with clients."

"We'll get caught up today. Give me thirty minutes to clear my desk, then send in the first victim." I grinned at her.

"You got it."

I spent all day seeing clients. It was exhausting listening to the facts of each case, thinking about the issues, and outlining an approach and theory for every one. Most of the cases I took were not complex but, they were not without their specific set of problems and resolutions.

Sherry left at five. At six-thirty, I gathered my files and left the office.

Chapter Thirteen

The sidewalk was barren of people. Everyone had gone home to be with their families or hit the neighborhood watering holes. I sat in my car for a few minutes. No one seemed to be about, so I started the engine and left. I'd be on time—what a small miracle. It seemed that I was always running behind these days. An occupational hazard, no less. I entered the parking lot of the stadium at my old high school, and there he was, sitting at the fifty-yard line, waiting. My breath quickened, and my body felt like the heat of a thousand Julys. I hated this. I couldn't feel this way. Swallowing was difficult, and I took deep breaths before I got out of the car. Just talk business, Micki, I lectured myself.

"Waiting long?" I kept my voice calm.

"Not long. Thanks for coming."

"Not a problem. So what is your problem?" I was a bit nervous.

"It's not an easy story."

"First of all, is this privileged communication?"

"What do you mean?" He looked confused.

"I mean, are you speaking to me as an attorney?"

"Yes, definitely. I want you to be my lawyer."

"Why do you need a lawyer?"

"It's a long story. I hope you have some respect left for me once I've told you what I know. I am involving you partly because you worked for the lab when all of this started and I trust you. But mostly because I don't know any other lawyer who will understand both the police work and the forensic work involved."

"I'm listening." This was what I had been waiting for: an explanation of the recent events.

"I involved you in this case because you are already involved. Remember the Wayne Jeffries case?"

"Of course. Anna and I have come to the conclusion that Wayne's case is what this is all about."

"It's part of it, yes, but it goes much deeper. I don't know everything, I thought I did, but it's become obvious to me that I wasn't told the whole story. Your old boss knows the whole story. He's right smack in the middle of it, and he's disappeared, gone without a trace."

"What do you mean he's gone? Anna says he's been binging and disappearing for a few days at a time, sometimes as long as a week."

"He may be drinking, but I'm telling you he's gone, nowhere to be found. I know how to reach him at all times, and I can't find him. He's not at home and not at his beach cabin. His mobile phone and pager don't answer, not even his voice mail. I've done surveillance everywhere he frequents, and he hasn't been seen for three days."

"Why would he disappear?"

"I don't know, it's not like him. I think maybe he's fled the country. Or even worse, he's dead.He didn't take anything with him, and his car is still in his garage. I checked that out first."

"What?" I was in shock.

"The word around the precinct is that the FBI is looking for him, but maybe someone else got to him before they did."

"I don't get it."

Chapter Fourteen

"It all started not long after the mistrial, when Jake got off. It was the summer you left for law school. Bob called me in August of 1987 to meet him at a downtown bar, near the police station. He said it would be worth my while. It wouldn't take long, and it would further my career, so I went. When I got there, he was drunk, as usual. He told me to sit down. Then he asked me if I'd like to be chief of police. I told him I would, but it would take a while.

"He said it wouldn't, if I played my cards right. All I had to do was forget that I submitted certain evidence to the lab that never made it to the first trial and other evidence that damn sure wouldn't make it to a retrial.

"I asked him why, and all he'd say was that it would make someone very happy. In return I could become chief while I was still young.

"When I asked him what was missing from the first trial, he told me not to trouble myself about that. I still remember his words, 'Roy, it's over and done, and you testified righteously.'

"I told him I wouldn't sabotage any retrial, that my ethics were better than that and he knew it. Then he started talking about ambition. I told him that I was ambitious, but not enough to break the law to get what I wanted. He said I wouldn't really have to break the law, it would just be a sin of omission.

"I asked what he would get out of it and he said it was money, a lot of money, enough to retire on. He wouldn't have to smell any more dead bodies—and something about not having to hang around in the swamp much longer either. He told me I didn't have much of a choice in the matter, that he was trying to make it an attractive offer because the dark side was grim.

"I said I did have a choice and that I wouldn't interfere with an investigation or tamper with evidence. Then Bob said I would if I wanted to stay healthy. It was go along and be chief, or be dead. I couldn't believe it and said he was just a drunk—who was pulling his strings? According to him it wasn't anybody I knew— and what was it going to be?

"I got pissed and told him to fuck off. He just said if I didn't cooperate my children's shiny faces wouldn't be so shiny any more. Then I really couldn't believe it. He said it wasn't his style, but the people he was protecting wouldn't hesitate to harm them. All I had to do was be a good sport and go along, I didn't have anything to lose if I just went along.

"Then I sort of gave up, because he'd have my kids and me killed if I didn't.

"He said he was just a messenger and I reminded him about the messenger getting shot. He told me he was willing to take the risk, it was worth it.

"Something in Bob's face told me he was scared. He lacked his usual obnoxious confidence. His voice quivered when he threatened me. He squirmed, cracked his knuckles, tapped his fingers, and twitched all the time we were talking. As greedy as he was, I knew he was scared.

"Then he told me not to go anywhere for a while. I was to be available to him if he called me. And especially I wasn't to talk to anybody because it wouldn't be wise. Something about it would complicate matters and I'd get blood on my hands and my conscience would bother me. I had to watch out so my over-active do-gooder gene didn't kick in.

"I told him I heard him loud and clear, but he better sober up, because he'd need all his wits about him if his retirement program went haywire. He could wind up in a witness protection program, or worse. When I heard myself say that, I finally realized that Bob wasn't kidding."

When Roy finished his story he sighed.

"That was it, and then I left. I couldn't get away from that son-of-a-bitch fast enough. I've been waiting thirteen years for the case to be retried. It's like waiting for the other shoe to drop. The year 2000 hasn't been too good to me so far."

I looked at Roy before I responded. I couldn't imagine Roy living with Bob's threat all of these years. I wondered if this is what caused the breakup of Roy's marriage. Who could live with the stress? Maybe he intentionally distanced himself from his wife and children to protect them.

Then I spoke. "He's even scummier than I thought. Until now, I hated him because he hated women, used women, wouldn't hire anyone but women so he could oppress them. He was a drunk and a scoundrel, he was immoral, and he was selfish."

"He's much more sinister than any of that, Micki."

"So what's happened since you met with him? That was a long time ago."

"Nothing, just a few reminder phone calls. You know, cryptic messages that no one but he and I would understand. He's afraid of wiretapping. The paranoid fucker."

"He's always been paranoid. That's why I can't believe that he would go along with anything like this. Someone has something on him. He's too chicken-shit, a real coward—and cowards don't volunteer."

"I've never liked the guy, so I don't know much about his personal life. Just my luck that I happen to be the detective on this murder case all those years ago. I wouldn't wish this on my worst enemy."

"Anyone else work this case with you?"

"No, just me. Wait a minute—a guy from the sheriff's office was involved at the beginning. There was a question regarding whether Wayne lived inside or outside the city limits, so the county sheriff's office sent someone over the day after the crime to look over the evidence. The jurisdiction issue resolved itself once we checked Wayne's tax records."

"Who was it? Do I know him? Did he come to the lab to view the evidence?"

"No, I checked the evidence out for him to inspect at my office. You never dealt with him. I figured he would never factor into the trial anyway, because the city had jurisdiction of the case after all. The city annexed the part of the county where Wayne's acreage was located years ago. I really never thought about him much after that. He was a new guy, and I didn't know him very well. I think his name was Billy—yes, Billy Shipley."

"Where is he now?" I asked.

"I think he transferred or something, right before the trial."

"You'd better look into his whereabouts. He may know something that you don't."

"I don't see how. The county's involvement was cut short. I can't imagine why the sheriff's office would have continued to be involved once it was determined we had control over the case."

"That's the point. When did they decide that they were out of it?"

"I don't remember, but I can ask around. I'll have to be careful about it. I think we're all being watched."

"Who is we?"

"You, me, Anna, Bob—anyone involved directly or indirectly with this case."

I shook my head in disbelief. "Great, I've been gone almost thirteen years, and I'm involved. Just great."

"I'd give anything not to involve you. God, I hate this. I've always done the best job I possibly could. Never skirted the edge, if you know what I mean—and look at my reward."

"I know you never crossed over to the other side doing undercover work, and it's admirable. So many fall from grace, so many the public never hears about."

Roy stood up, his body limp and his head bent forward. "I feel so helpless and ashamed. Please don't be disappointed in me, Micki. All I ever really wanted was your love and respect."

"You have my respect, and I'm not disappointed in you. You haven't done anything wrong, have you? The case was never retried."

"I haven't done anything to right this situation."

"What can you do?"

"I don't know."

"Who do you know that you could trust with this?"

"No one. That's why I haven't told anyone but you."

"Oh, I feel much better." I couldn't help being sarcastic. I was still suspicious about Roy's intentions and his persistence in drawing me deeper into the case.

"Sorry, but I feel better. You know how it is, it eases your mind to tell someone else your problems."

"Yes, if the world is your therapist. You better keep your mouth shut until we think of someone who can help us. It won't be the police department or the sheriff's office or the FBI. Offhand, I can't think of anyone we can trust with this. Better let it unravel as it may. But, I warn you if anyone comes after my child, my husband, or me, you'll be sorry."

"So far all of us are still breathing, except maybe Bob. If one of us has to go, let it be him."

"Ain't that the truth," I agreed. "Hey, Roy, I'm proud of you. I always have been, even when I was mad at you. Don't worry about your position in this, just keep up your good habits. Aristotle said, 'We are what we repeatedly do. Excellence, then, is not an act, but a habit.'"

"Do you think I'm excellent?" He smiled at me.

"I don't know, I haven't tried you."

It was a comment that slipped out, but it altered the mood of our meeting. I looked down after I realized what I had said, and he turned his head sideways, leaned over, and looked into my eyes.

"Would you like to try me? I'd love to try you."

"I'm married now, Roy."

"Since when has that ever stopped you from doing what you really wanted to do?"

"Since I made a promise to Les that I intend to keep. Even if I am weak, even if I am curious, and even if it hurts like crazy to sit here with you and maintain control. I grew up, and I don't look for love in all the wrong places anymore. Besides I found someone who makes me feel what I need to feel, in and out of bed."

"I'll wait. I've been waiting this long, I'll wait forever—or however long it takes. Because I think you're worth waiting for. I care about you, it's not just the sex."

"Don't take advantage of my marital situation right now. I know you know Les is away, and this case bonds us, at least temporarily."

"Yes, it does. But I won't take advantage. I promise."

"Just remember our being thrown together working this case is situational."

"I know it is, and I don't want you that way. I'll wait until you want me too."

"You're pretty sure about this, aren't you?"

"You're home to me. No one else is. I've waited for you to come back. You belong here, and nowhere else. You fit, I fit, we fit together. I'm not saying I've been celibate, but there hasn't been anyone I've felt anything for."

"That's sad."

"I don't mean to depress you."

"You're not, but it makes me stop and think about where I've been and what I've learned since I came back. There has been such love, such joy in my life, that I can't imagine anyone not having had the same love and joy. Besides, you didn't value me so much when I was available to you."

"Not everyone takes their chances. Not everyone lands on their feet. Sometimes life passes you by because you don't know how to jump on."

"Well, one thing I've learned is that it's the little things in life that matter. The small, good things. Very few people in this world realize greatness, so it is very important to live each day as if it were special. I've also learned that it's not the beginnings or the endings that count, but the middle that really matters. I learned this after my divorce, and now I live by it."

"I guess we've all grown up some since you left."

"I hope so. I've got to get home now. Let me know what you find out about Bob—and call me if you need a lawyer. Don't wait too long, and if you're contacted directly by the FBI, I want to know about it immediately."

"You'll be the first one I call. Thanks again for listening to me."

"Sure, I can be a good listener."

"Be careful going home. The feds are controlling the case and don't know who to follow, but I'm sure the bad guys do, whoever they are. We're at a real disadvantage not knowing who the bad guys are. You can bet if I find Bob, I'm going to beat the information out of him."

I wondered why Roy hadn't beaten the crap out of Bob when he first heard the story.

"Don't hurt him too bad. He doesn't look like much of a fighter."

"Drunks never are. He'll talk if I find him. This has all gone a little too far. He's involved innocent people for nothing more than his greed. The more I think about it, the madder I get."

"Remember, Roy, his character has been genetically defective since day one. He doesn't care about anyone but himself, so it makes the rest of us more vulnerable. Bob is more cowardly than he is greedy."

"If he's dead, we may never know the whole story."

"Let's hope he surfaces, and soon. I have a feeling that this is all beginning to escalate, and I want us to be prepared when it does."

"You and me both, girl."

"I want my life and my hard-earned career intact when all the dust settles. I've worked too hard and come too far to let that greedy coward and your badge compromise my accomplishments. I'll be your lawyer, but I don't like the fact you involved me in something dangerous. I love my family. You'd better protect them at all costs."

"I will, Micki. I promise." Roy promised a lot lately.

Chapter Fifteen

I walked slowly to my car. We didn't leave together. Sliding behind the wheel, I started the engine, then I left. Old memories washed over me, fond and not so fond, cool football weather, a winning team, a jealous boyfriend, good friends, and a sense of lost youth. I drove home in a daydream. When I saw my driveway, I didn't remember how I got home. Washed out and weary, I hated the thought of being alone.

Where was Jorge? He usually came to greet me when I got home. I hoped he was all right. He was all I had in the form of male companionship.

Lord, don't let me be one of those women who replaces men with cats. Somehow I didn't think that would ever happen. I liked men, always had.

I'd call Les—that would make me feel better. The house was warm so I turned on the air conditioner and looked toward the back yard for Jorge. There he was, sitting under our largest pecan tree. "Come on in, Jorge." He came meowing a story of sorts that I couldn't understand, but it sounded cheerful, and I needed that. I loved my cat and took good care of him. He had a great veterinarian, and I couldn't count the times I had rescued him from fights. He put on a show, but he wasn't much of a fighter.

My evening hours were filled with the little tasks that married couples fight over and live-in couples avoid doing altogether. After washing the dishes, taking out the trash, and folding clothes, I finished up the evening with a turkey sandwich, a glass of Diet Coke, and some paperwork from the office. I watched enough television to bore me, then turned off the light and tried to sleep.

I did sleep, but I had anxiety dreams. What happened to the sleep of angels that I had before practicing law and having a baby? I had drifted off to sleep when I dreamed that a skeleton of some sort was chasing Anna, on foot no less. She looked terrified. She was running like her life depended on it. Someone was calling her name, she didn't look back, she kept running, further and further into the woods. She ran until I couldn't see her anymore. I tried to help her, but I couldn't find her. Where had she gone?

When I awoke it was three A.M., and a verse of the Robert Frost poem was running through my head, "The woods are lovely, dark, and deep, but I have promises to keep, and miles to go before I sleep, and miles to go before I sleep." It was eerie, the dream and the poem. I was perspiring and shaking. Why was this happening? It felt as though my whole universe had turned upside down since the day I entered the old mansion. Where did I go from here? I lay in bed for three hours and contemplated my next move. No one was going to tell me anything, I didn't belong with law enforcement anymore, they didn't trust lawyers anyway. I'd have to depend on Anna and Roy. It would be up to them to find Bob—make some sense of this frantic madness and restore some peace in our lives.

Tuesday morning my phone rang. It was Anna.

"We having dinner tonight?"

"Yes, I think I'll cook this creole dish with cioppino sauce."

"I'll eat anything as long as I don't have to cook it. Can I bring something?"

"Bring your favorite bottle of wine. I have a bottle, but we may need two." I giggled.

"Certainly. We'll need at least two bottles." Anna emphasized the *two*.

"I saw Roy yesterday."

"Oh, really. Whatever for?"

"Not what you think, but I'll tell you about it once you get here. You know how I feel about discussing criminal cases over the phone."

"Can't be too careful. Things have gotten strange this past week. Have you had any insect problems lately?"

"I'm not sure. I haven't sprayed for bugs in awhile. Maybe I'll call the exterminators this week."

"Be sure that you do."

"See you tonight."

"I'll be there with bells on."

I hadn't even thought about my home being bugged, but it made sense. After all, who would have known about my trip with Jean to Shelby? Yes, there must be at least one bug here. I tip-toed over to the phone in the kitchen, unscrewed the receiver. Nothing there. I went to the family room, checked the phone there. Nothing again. Finally, I inspected the phone in the master bedroom, and there it was: a listening device. Fuckety-fuck-fuck-fuck. Why didn't I think to check this as soon as I got home two days ago? I didn't think in those terms anymore, not since I left law enforcement. Now it was evident that I was in this as deep as the others.

After a quick shower, minimal makeup, and a toaster strudel, it was time to leave for work. Only two more days, and then I left for cooler, drier weather. Les and Michael and I would become the funny trinity again. I hoped whoever bugged my home would leave my family alone. They already knew where Les and Michael were.

The drive to work was relaxing, thanks to the small town of Liberty. Sherry was waiting for me with a stack of files. It was our weekly morning meeting on cases. We discussed where we were, where we needed to be, and what needed immediate atten-tion. She announced the name at the top of each file, stated what had been accomplished on each case, and what was yet to be done this week, if anything.

"What are you going to do with Mr. Meyers, the pervert?" she inquired.

"He disappears on a regular basis, a real slippery guy. His pretrial is set next week, let's reset it for next month. Tell the judge we can't locate him at this time, and that I'll be out of town at the end of the week. If we can't find him during the next two weeks, then I'll withdraw from his case."

While normal folk were watching *Indecent Proposal*, I was working on Mr. Meyer's case of indecent exposure. Criminal defense work paralleled my old job at the crime lab. While your average citizen was in church on Sunday morning, I was looking at dead bodies in rice fields, back yards, cars, homes, and wooded areas.

Sherry and I reviewed about forty cases, and finally she came to the last three winners, those that I'd been appointed by the court to represent. One was a case on appeal where the defendant was given a life sentence for driving while intoxicated. He was a habitual criminal, and it seemed that the jury took a disliking to him when he clucked like a chicken throughout the entire trial. The judge appointed me to the retrial. His previous attorney had, "Reasonable Doubt for a Reasonable Fee" printed on his business card. He completely lacked the ability to back up his slogan.

Next was a court appointed murder case; and I had co-counsel on that one. A Mexican—illegal alien—had been found floating in the Neches River with approximately forty stab wounds. Two brothers were the suspects.

Last, but not least, I was finally finishing an appointed federal case, my third one this year. I now know why people say, "Don't make a federal case out of it." Federal cases are the worst. The defendants are a whole different breed of criminal, and the process is expedited beyond belief in comparison to the state system. The judges can be real assholes because they have life tenure. The juries resemble the characters from *Deliverance*. You know the ones.

I mean really, what jury of your peers? Federal jurors are drawn from the most rural areas in the state of Texas. I mean rural with a capital R. If your peers are red-neck farmers, ranchers, inbred cousins, uninformed, uneducated white folk who hate everybody except their own kind, then you're in luck. If you are one of the rest of us, then you get to spend the rest of your natural life in a federal penitentiary somewhere, compliments of a federal jury. My door opening slightly jarred me from my daymare. One of my favorite clients, a pixieish little girl I had gotten to know while doing her adoption, stood there.

"Hello, Shelly, how are you today?"

"Fine, ma'am," the six-year-old responded shyly.

"Are your mother and your father-to-be here?"

"They're out there." She pointed toward the waiting room.

I saw Sherry heading toward the waiting room to greet them.

As Emma and Kyle sat in the waiting room, Shelly crawled up in a chair in my office. I asked her a few preliminary questions before the hearing.

"Do you want Kyle to be your Daddy?"

"Yes, I like him a lot."

"What kinds of things do you do together?"

"Well, we go places together, we work in the garden, and cook, and play."

"Is he nice to you and your mother?"

"He's very nice, and he loves us very much."

"How do you feel when you are with him?"

"I feel good. No one can hurt me when Kyle is around."

"That's nice, Shelly. Is there anything that you want to ask me before we go to court and make Kyle your new Daddy?"

Shelly responded fretfully, "Will he always be my daddy?"

"He will always be your daddy."

"Good, because mamma needs him, and I do too."

"Well, let's gather everyone together and make this dream come true."

We walked toward the waiting room and I greeted the Broussards.

"Are we ready for this very special occasion?" I asked.

"More than ready," responded Mr. Broussard with a happy smile.

As we walked across the street, I reflected to a short while ago when Shelly was testifying before a grand jury about the sexual abuse bestowed upon her by her own biological father. I shuddered, then took a very deep breath, a cleansing breath, and felt much better. Her biological father's parental rights had been terminated, and he was spending the next ten years in prison. He would never be able to hurt her again. By the time he got out, she would be sixteen. She had received counseling for the past two years, and seemed much better. Her mother had remarried a man who was kind, generous, and loving. He would make a wonderful father to Shelly and the new baby they were expecting in October.

"Here we are, now have a seat right here on the front row, and I will tell the judge that we are all present." The guardian ad litem was speaking to the court reporter, and I greeted him.

"Everything all right with the social study, Joe?"

"Perfect."

"They're a wonderful couple, and they'll make a great family. Did you know that they're having a baby boy in the fall?"

"Yes, as a matter of fact, Shelly told me. Who could hurt such a sweet little girl?"

"All rise," the bailiff announced. The courtroom fell silent.

The judge had entered the courtroom.

"In the Interest of S.O.L., a minor child, is the petitioner ready?" the judge asked. Only Shelly's initials were used in the adoption documents to protect the privacy of the process.

"Yes, your honor, and all the appropriate parties are present and ready," I responded.

"Counsel, are you ready to proceed with the evidence?"

"Yes, your honor."

"Good. Will everyone approach the bench, please."

We all took our respective places, and everyone was sworn in. The court reporter took down the evidence, and at the close of the case, the judge turned to Shelly and said: "Young lady, your name is now officially Shelly Ollene Broussard. Are you happy about that?"

"Yes, your highness," she said in a whisper.

We all chuckled, including your highness.

"You can call me judge, Shelly."

"Okay, judge."

"I like your new name, Shelly. I'm only sorry that I could-n't improve on your initials. They might change when you get married."

We all snickered because we had already discussed Shelly's

initials changing from SOL to SOB. Of course, Shelly didn't understand. We all left the courtroom and walked to the district clerk's office to finalize the paperwork and record the appropriate documents. Once that was completed, everyone hugged and left the courthouse. The Broussards left arm in arm, the three of them. As usual, I left alone and headed back to my office to finish up the day.

"Back again. Any fires?" I asked Sherry.

"No, it's been unusually quiet. Here are the pretrial motions I typed while you were in court. You better look over them before I file them with the clerk."

She handed me the pretrial motions in the Meyers case, and I walked into my office, kicked off my heels, put my tired feet up on the desk, very ladylike, and proofread the motions. No typos, she's a wonder. I couldn't type a single line without errors. I hoped I wasn't wasting my time working on the Meyers case. If he disappeared again, I would have wasted investigator's time, secretarial time, and my own. I hoped he'd surface soon. I'd never withdrawn from a case in my entire career, but I would if I had to. It wouldn't bother me a bit to drop his sexual assault of a child case.

"Looking good," I said as I handed them back to Sherry. "Go ahead and file them. We can only hope he shows up soon—and reset his case while you're at the courthouse, please."

"Done deal. I'll put the phones on the answering service and be right back."

"I'll be here for another hour or so," I said.

The library was summoning me, legal research awaited. There were a few remaining problems to solve in the federal case I was working on.

The last court-appointed case I completed in the federal system was a drug case that took me over a year to resolve, with quite admirable results, I might add. The court-appointed system paid me one thousand dollars. Can you imagine? All of those jail visits, one hundred miles round-trip from my office, endless collect telephone calls from the client, pretrial motions with supporting briefs, and countless hearings and court appearances. I think I'll surrender my federal license, it had become a real pain in the ass. That drug case nearly shut down my state court practice last year. I couldn't risk that happening again.

Upon her return, Sherry found me in the law library.

"All filed," she said. "Aren't you having dinner guests tonight?"

"One guest. My good friend from the crime lab."

"How is Anna? She hasn't called the office lately."

"She's great," I lied.

"Any developments on that case you've been working on with Anna?"

"We've found a few things, what they mean I can't say."

I hated not telling her the full truth, but I was determined not to involve her. She was my lifeline in the office, and I didn't want her preoccupied or placed in any danger.

I changed the subject. "What time is it?"

"Five-thirty. Why?"

"Time for you to go home, and me too."

"You're leaving early today, boss." She raised her eyebrows in surprise.

"I know, but I have to go the grocery store, fix a cajun dish, and chill the wine before Anna arrives for dinner at seven."

"Maybe you should pick up something already prepared?"

"I'll be home by six, and that gives me an hour to get everything going."

"Well, have a good evening and a good dinner. Don't drink too much wine. Remember, one more day in the office this week. It could be hairy."

"Let's hope it's calm and productive. I'll be in court at nine sharp, call me on my digital phone if you need me. I should be back in the office by eleven or so."

Chapter Sixteen

I left the office right behind Sherry. No traffic this afternoon, what a relief. The small grocery store I frequented was close to the house, and everyone there knew me, from the owner to the bag boys. One of the bag boys followed me home a couple of weeks ago. He was quite embarrassed when I explained to him that I was forty years old, married, and had a young son. It seemed that he and some of his buddies thought I was younger and readily available. He didn't follow me home anymore after that.

I collected the few items I needed, paid the cashier, and rushed out the door. Again, I didn't remember the drive home. I was getting absentminded while driving.

I usually operated on automatic pilot once I started the engine. It must have been the sleep deprivation. I needed to be extra careful. The garage door raised for my car to enter and Jorge came skittering around the corner of the house. His back was arched and he was hissing. He ran past me and up a tree in the front yard. I figured a dog was chasing him.

As I unlocked the back door, I found myself face to face with a stranger wearing a mask. Before I had time to scream I was knocked to the floor. Terrified, I scrambled to my feet, grabbed my purse, and fished out my handgun. I had just started carrying a gun again. It was too late. He was gone. Gun in hand, I backed my car out of the driveway, tires screeching, and the steering wheel spinning. I drove around the block several times, circling the surrounding neighborhood, but no intruder. Slowly, I proceeded back home.

This was not going to be any burglar. It was related to the Jeffries case. All I could make of the intruder was that he appeared to have a small build, blonde hair tucked up under a cap, and was about five feet five inches. He wore a jogging suit and tennis shoes—an unusual combination with the baseball cap.

I walked around back and found where the intruder entered. A broken pane in the french doors. He had reached through once he broke it and unlocked the deadbolt. I'm getting a keyed deadbolt first thing tomorrow. Next, I eased into the house, gun clutched to my breast, cat in tow, and found nothing disturbed, thank goodness. That would have been the final straw. I called Roy, he wasn't in. I hesitated, then left a message for him to return my call.

Maybe a shower would restore my sanity and erase my emotional turmoil. Warm water trickled down my body, and carnal thoughts bubbled around in my brain, like a glass of champagne. I realized that I was thinking about Roy—his tempting smile, his salt-and-pepper hair, his blue eyes, his twisted sense of humor, his undercover work, and, last but not least, his lust for me.

It aroused me to acknowledge how much he wanted me, but wanted me for what? Sex? Companionship? Entertainment? What? I reminded myself that I didn't trust him. My arousal subsided somewhat, but not altogether. I missed him and I needed to see him, but I couldn't before I left for Colorado. I didn't need the confusion, though I was convinced that Roy and I were destined to have an emotional and reckless ending, no matter what.

My body tingled and I was excited thinking about what it would be like to make love with him. Sex with Roy would be urgent, very oral. Traditional and not so traditional—an all-nighter. I realized I might need a cold shower if I kept on thinking about sex with Roy.

In the distance I heard my phone ringing. It was Anna. Her

house had been burglarized. Strange. Her place was ransacked, but nothing was missing. Evidently the intruder hit her first, and then I interrupted him. We agreed that it would take someone really stupid to break in at a time when people come home from work. And that we were having dinner anyway. She would just check for insects — she could clean up later.

I tidied up my place, and about six-thirty, I dressed casually in a sundress — no bra of course, I hated them. I only wore them to work. Next I pulled out all the kitchen utensils I would need, put the wine in the freezer, and got to work. Somehow I didn't believe that forgetting the wine would be a problem tonight.

Anna arrived promptly at seven. When I let her in, she was carrying two bottles of vino.

"Micki, where was your bug?"

"In the bedroom phone."

"Did you keep it?"

"You bet your sweet ass I kept it. Did you check your phones?" I asked.

"Nothing in my phones, but I found a listening device set up in my attic. You know how the feds love those, they pick up any conversation you have in your entire house."

"What made you look up there?"

"It happened a while back in another case. By the way, Roy called me over the lab car radio and wanted me to check on you. He's out on a drug bust, and he can't get back to you for awhile. What did Roy have to say yesterday, other than he's hot for your body?"

"He told me a very scary story, but I can't tell you, because it's privileged. I can tell you after we dug up that evidence at the beach, Roy panicked. An old threat came back to haunt him. He wants me to be his lawyer, and he's convinced that this case is going to blow up in his face and ruin his career — or even worse, take his life."

"Jesus Christ, what's happening here?"

"I don't know, but you and Roy better find out quick, find out before the dumb-ass FBI does. Once they get entrenched in this case, we're all fucked. The FBI only gets involved if the stakes are high. The corruption must run pretty high up the ladder."

"You said a mouthful."

"Let's get dinner and we'll talk while we eat," I suggested.

We worked in silence for awhile, drank a couple of glasses of wine, then sat down to eat. Our bowls were full of spicy shrimp and rice, covered in a creole sauce.

"Did you learn to cook while you were away?"

"No, I've been cooking since I was nineteen, but never had anyone to cook for when I worked at the lab. No reason to cook for one person, is there?"

"No reason at all. I haven't cooked since Harry left town. Micki, he may take a permanent job out of town next year. He's gotten quite a reputation conducting the marijuana eradication programs. That's why he's been gone a lot lately. He's trying to finish up his narcotics cases before he retires from the Department of Public Safety. This job out of town would be low-key and the perfect semi-retirement job for him. He would be training law enforcement individuals in drug detection."

"I would miss you terribly."

"You could visit often. I want to retire too. After this career case, I'll be more than ready. Not to change the subject, Micki, but tell me what Roy said about Bob. Nothing that interferes with your attorney-client privilege, but anything that will help me solve this mystery."

"I can give you generalities and anything the lab should legally know. Let me think — Bob's into something seedy, and he's trying to pull Roy down with him. It appears that Bob is trying very hard to retire a wealthy man, and someone is paying him to conceal evidence in the Jeffries case. Bob wants certain evidence to disappear so that the case can't be reopened."

"Was something missing during the first trial?"

"Evidently. You'll be the one to determine that since you have access to the evidence from the prior trial. I can help you with what may be missing, because I testified in the first trial. I know what was admitted into evidence at the trial from our laboratory. What I don't know is what may have initially disappeared from the lab vault when it was submitted by the police department. Only the evidence technician, or possibly you may have seen something come in to the lab later that disappeared before it was ever analyzed and reported back to the DA's office. Or maybe, the evidence was never submitted at all. In that case, we'll never know what disappeared."

"I'll make a list of everything we have on the case, and I'll let you know. So the boss is looking to go out a rich man?"

" 'Go out' may be right if he doesn't watch himself. Roy seems to think that the FBI is here to investigate the lab and the law enforcement agencies that were involved in this case. He also thinks that the feds have an informant who has provided sufficient evidence on the old murder case to reopen the investigation. We've got to find out what's going on before they do, or some of us could be hurt, or even killed. According to Roy, there is a sophisticated conspiracy behind the old murder. The feds have the uncanny ability to open a can of worms, and then watch them all dry out and die."

Anna jumped from her chair. "Micki, let's go check the lab right now."

"I can't go with you. If Bob found out, he would have my ass."

"What can he do to you? If he finds out he may not like it, but if what you're saying is true, who would he tell?"

"You're right. He can't tell a soul, and he may be dead for all we know. I'll do it. Either way, I'm doing this to help out a friend. After all, I was the testifying chemist. You're lucky to be a non-testifying lab technician, or else whoever has Bob by the balls would have you as well."

Chapter Seventeen

When we got to the lab, it was already very dark. My heart was double beating in my chest as Anna pulled into the underground parking garage of the police department. She leapt from the car and unlocked the basement door where the crime lab was located. Anna unlocked and relocked another series of doors behind us.

"Do you think anyone is watching us, Anna?"

"I didn't see anyone follow us here, and I was damn sure watching after that incident this afternoon."

She turned on the light in the lab, walked into the back room, and opened the vault. The log book was near the entry of the vault, and she looked up the lab number corresponding to the evidence she was searching for.

"Here it is."

"What's in the envelope?" I asked.

"Not much. There must have been more."

"Hell, yes, there was more. Remember the nine millimeter we found at the beach and the shells—they're not here. The submission form and everything is missing. Bob must have taken it, buried it at the beach near his cabin, and figures what? That no one will miss it. What's he going to say to the feds when they ask him where the evidence is? Or maybe he plans to be long gone before the investigation is completed or the case is retried."

"I'm sure that's it. He's been paid off, and he's long gone."

"I'm not so sure. Whoever it is that has the money also has a vested interest in not getting caught. Bob would be the one to tidy up any loose ends and answer any questions asked about the missing evidence."

"What else is missing?"

"Offhand, I can't think of anything but the gun—the bullets, some fingerprint cards, and the shoes. Yes, there were shoes found at the defendant's house and later submitted to the lab for comparison. I found a bloody shoe-print at the murder scene, and the defendant's shoe was matched to that bloody print."

"If the evidence was so strong, why did the case end in a mistrial?"

"The District Attorney screwed up. He was young and green. He made a prejudicial statement in front of the jury. In open court, he called Jake Edmonds, the defendant, a liar and a murderer. He also made references to Jake's criminal history, which included a prior incarceration for burglary. Judge Herman declared a mistrial. The judge had no choice—you can't call the defendant a liar or a murderer in front of a jury. It was like throwing a skunk in the jury box, then asking them not to smell it. There was no way to cure the error. The odd thing is that the case has never been retried. The judge emphatically informed the jury that the case would go to trial again. As a matter of fact, he said he'd see to it personally. He was seething when he said it. He was sick of the District Attorney's cavalier attitude."

"Micki, Judge Herman died less than a year after Wayne was murdered."

"That might explain why the case was never retried. The DA didn't want to revisit it, and the new sitting judge was unfamiliar with the facts."

"The only items left in evidence are Wayne's bloody clothing, the gun powder residue swabs taken from Wayne's hands, photographs, and a few hairs and fibers. That's not much."

I exhaled slowly. "Not enough for a new trial, that's a certainty."

"What else was in the vault during the first trial?"

"Just what we have here, and the stuff we dug up at the beach."

"So, if Bob tampered with the evidence, it was before you ever analyzed it?"

"Either that, or the evidence never made it to the lab." I was emphatic.

"So now we have to make a decision. We have the other evidence, maybe not all of it, but we have what they originally went to trial with."

"Where do we go from here?"

Anna looked at me. "We aren't telling the FBI, are we?"

"Hell, no. They're such screwups, they're probably the ones who followed me to Shelby and ransacked your house. We're probably suspects as far as they're concerned. They'd turn on their own mothers if they thought it would get them publicity."

"They followed you to Shelby? You didn't tell me that."

"I called you from Shelby, but you weren't home. I was going to tell you tonight, and then it sort of slipped my mind."

"Do you really think it was them?"

"You bet I do, now that I think about it. They didn't tail me very well, and someone with more expertise would have been a better tail. The goofballs think that we're involved, and why not? Our scumbag director is missing. We're the only ones left for them to torture. They know less than we do. Isn't that comforting?"

"It wouldn't surprise me if they arrested both of us."

"They don't have enough information. But don't worry. If they want to harass someone, it will be me. I took some shots at them when they followed me."

"You didn't?"

"They scared me and Jean pretty bad. She's probably home right now taking Nyquil so she can sleep tonight."

"Why would they involve her?"

"They probably didn't mean to. She just got in the way, and they didn't care."

"Let's get out of here before someone sees us. We can talk about it on the way home." Anna was pleading.

She replaced the evidence where she found it and locked the vault.

I had an idea. "Anna, check Bob's desk and see if he's been here lately."

"Nope. The same lab reports are sitting on his desk waiting for his signature. As far as I can tell, nothing has been moved."

We worked our way down the dark hall with a flashlight from the lab. It was Anna's idea not to turn on any lights while we were leaving the building. Once in the car, we discussed what we knew and more so what we didn't know.

"We have the evidence from the first murder trial, even though Bob doesn't know we do. Roy knows about this. Any reason to think he may be dirty?" Anna asked.

"I don't think so. I hope not."

"We'll know if he is. After all, only the three of us know where both envelopes of evidence are. I have the beach evidence locked up tight in the vault."

"We have the gun, the bullets, the shirt, the gun powder residue swabs, hairs, fibers, and no shoes. They must have been taken before the first trial."

"Can you think of anything else that's missing?"

"I believe some fingerprints I lifted at the scene are missing."

"And we have the items that I collected from the mansion—the other gun, more bullets, the gloves, keys, and an unidentified body. Not to mention blood stains, hair, fibers, and a whole butt-load of other trace evidence."

"I know. Where will you begin?"

"Well, the body will be identified by the pathologist by early next week. First I'll look at the gun, the bullets, and the blood to see if they are connected to the body. You know that gun is a nine millimeter, just like the one from the beach.

"You know who carries nine millimeters, don't you?" I raised my eyebrows.

"The cops," Anna replied.

"Don't discuss the results with anyone except me. I'll be back from Colorado by the time you have anything to report."

"On Monday?"

"Absolutely. Any chance you'll have results during the next two days?"

"No way. I have evidence to test on six drug cases going to

trial, not to mention a hit and run, two aggravated sexual assault cases, and another murder case waiting for analysis. The DA is screaming for results on all of them. It will take me a good three days, and maybe the weekend as well. I'll meet you on Monday if I have anything to tell you."

"No more talking over the phone. Great big ears are listening."

At Anna's, everything was as she left it. We picked up a little before she took me home. It was hard to tell what the idiots were looking for, but we were assuming that they didn't find it.

We drove off listening to *Creedence Clearwater Gold*. It brought back memories of a concert I worked with Roy, unintentionally, of course. It was his idea of a date. He was funny that way. It was as if law enforcement was his occupation, his preoccupation, his entertainment, and his paramour.

When I got home, there was a message from Les on my recorder. He would meet me at the Denver airport tomorrow night. I didn't need to call him back. I packed my warm clothing as quickly as possible. It was still cold in the Uncompahgre National Forest that Les loved so much.

I looked around. It still gave me the willies to think that some-one tried to break in, and it infuriated me to know that the place was bugged, more than likely by my old nemesis, the FBI.

When my brothers and I were kids, we used to say that FBI stood for " female body inspectors." I was convinced that the FBI was afflicted with a case of the dumb-ass and they suspected Anna and me because we worked the old Jeffries case together. How far off could they get? Well, not too far off. After all, Bob was involved. But the fed's incessant bunglings weren't going to aid the progress of this case one bit.

As a matter of fact, there could be deadly repercussions if the three of us couldn't put it together soon.

If this case was fatal, I wanted my headstone to read, "In Remembrance of Her Wit, Tenacity, and Passion." Of course, I also wanted a really expensive marble headstone with a huge angel on top. Oh, I was just being silly, I told myself. Nothing was going to happen to any of us. Anna—Bob, when he returned— would be slaving away while I was gone.

It was beginning to bother me that I was leaving town at this particular moment. I was afraid I'd miss something. I wanted to be right smack dab in the middle of it when it all came together.

I took a long walk before bedtime. Walking was part of my exercise regimen, and I did everything I could to put off lying down each night. Dreaming wasn't much fun these days. I started reading the trial transcript that Anna left me. She wouldn't have time for that, and it would be the last thing anybody looked at. There could be some clues, some real information in the documents. The first hundred pages or so was the voire dire of the jury.

The DA was lame, and the defense attorney wasn't much better. The defendant, a former employee of Wayne's, was most fortunate that the DA's office gave a pathetic performance. I had faith that a conviction might be possible in this new age of prosecution and technology. Even the lab was better equipped than it had been all those years ago. They had recently solved a thirty-one-year-old case with DNA evidence.

I read on past the opening statements, on to the prosecutor's direct examination of key witnesses, and the defense's cross-examination of these witnesses. Still no lead. I got bored, and then I drifted off to sleep. Before I knew it, the alarm was playing rock and roll music at an ungodly volume.

I marveled at the fact that I did not toss and turn all night. I ate a bite, dressed quickly, and ran out the door.

Chapter Eighteen

Last day at work. Hallelujah. While driving to work, I realized how unnerved I'd been since the boys left and, even more so, since the investigation of "Belle of the Bayou" began.

Sherry had coffee waiting when I arrived. She had become accustomed to me looking like something the cat dragged in these past few weeks, but she had been nice enough not to mention it.

"Last day. Are you packed and ready?"

"You bet, and as soon as we wrap up here today, I'm gone. I threw my luggage in the trunk before I left the house. Would you be a dear and drop me at the airport? I'll catch a cab back."

"Don't mind a bit."

"What's on the agenda this morning?"

"Well, guess who finally surfaced?"

"Mr. I-Can't-Keep-My-Pants-Zipped Meyers?"

"You guessed it, and he's frantic to see you."

"We got any time in the schedule today before I leave?"

"You have about an hour after lunch from two till three."

"Call him and have him come in. I need to talk to the little bastard before I leave. Sherry, once I finish proofreading and signing all these motions, please file them some time today."

"Yes, ma'am. What's on your agenda after that?"

"I have a meeting at the DA's office about ten that will take about two hours. I'll be back by lunchtime. Order me some take-out, nothing too fattening."

"Anything special I need to work on Thursday and Friday while you're out?"

"I'll leave you a list, and you know you can reach me on my digital while I'm away."

Sherry buried herself in word processing, and I got busy with paperwork. The hour passed quickly, and I left for my meeting at the courthouse. The meeting with the District Attorney of Liberty County was relevant to an aggravated assault case and its companion retaliation case, an alleged assault between two brothers. My client allegedly pulled a .22 caliber pistol on his brother, who called the police. Then my client allegedly retaliated by threatening the police when they arrived. I had sworn statements from witnesses stating that the incident involving the gun never occurred. A video of the arrest showed no retaliation or threat that I could see. It seemed that the two brothers fought because my client had called his brother a whining baby. But there was no weapon involved and to the best of my knowledge there were no injuries. A clear case of insufficient evidence. It was my job once my illustrious client was arrested to see that the case was not indicted. There was no case, just good old dysfunctional family feuding. They needed to get counseling and the book *Twelve Steps to a Dysfunctional Family Holiday*.

The meeting was productive and relatively painless. My client was to pay some restitution, and his cases would be declined for prosecution. It seemed fair enough, and I left the DA to return to my office. It was about eleven-thirty, and I checked my messages. There were a few from clients, and one from Roy. "Please meet me for lunch, noon at the Boondocks."

"Sherry, have you ordered lunch for me yet?"

"No, when I got that call about the lunch invitation, I canceled your order."

"What did you tell Roy?"

"I told him that you were in a meeting across the street, and you would be back around noon."

"Did you obligate me to this lunch?"

"He said you two had already talked about it. Did I do something wrong?"

"No, it's okay. Just clear it with me next time. This guy can really be persistent. I'll be back by one-thirty."

It was about a twenty-minute drive to the restaurant, and I wondered why Roy picked something so out-of-the-way. I guessed he had his reasons. When I got there, Roy was sitting in the back next to a window overlooking the bayou. There was a small crowd in the restaurant. It was quite a draw if you liked catfish and flounder. Catfish were found in the bayou, flounder were driven over by the locals who fished the cappuccino-colored Gulf of Mexico near Sabine Pass, which was just a few short miles away. I didn't see anyone I recognized but Roy.

"Hi. Glad you could make it."

"Did I have a choice?"

"You could have stood me up."

"That's not my style."

"I know, and I needed to see you. Micki, the pathologist's report is out, and the body we found at Belle has been identified."

"But Anna said it wouldn't be out until next week."

"The feds had the identification expedited."

"Who is it?"

"Remember the guy I told you about? The one from the sheriff's office who came to review the evidence after the Jeffries murder?"

"The guy I didn't know?"

"Yeah. Billy Shipley. Well, evidently someone knew him, someone who thought he knew too much."

The waiter interrupted our conversation. I let Roy order for me. Roy picked up where he left off. "We only met once, and then I never saw him again. Frankly he never crossed my mind since then."

"Did everyone assume that he was transferred or moved away?"

"I guess so. He must have been unattached while he worked here, or else someone in his family would have reported him missing."

"I wonder who got to him, and if Bob had anything to do with his demise?"

"I wonder that myself. Bob could have given him an ultimatum, like the one he gave me. Maybe the guy didn't think he was serious. After all, Billy didn't live in town long enough to know anyone very well."

"Roy, have you told anyone else about Billy's connection to the case?"

"No, I told you that we would keep all this between the three of us."

"I'm relieved to hear that. Another question for you: have you heard from Bob?"

"No. And I hope he's not dead, we may need his help."

"I've never needed help that bad, Roy."

"This time you might have to make an exception."

"That's a disgusting thought."

"There are too many unknown variables. With Wayne dead, he can't very well answer our questions."

"It's hard to think of Bob as being on our side," I said.

"I know. He's a scumbag. But if he's still alive, he's our man."

The waiter set a huge platter and two plates on our table.

"I'll be back to refill your tea glasses shortly," he mumbled and scurried away.

"So much for watching what I eat. Like my mom always says, 'even a two-by-four would be tasty if you fried it.'"

"She's right about that." Roy smacked his lips.

The waiter skirted around our table refilling our glasses. He was a jittery fellow.

"It's sad that Billy died because he didn't know enough about the bad guys to stay alive. You need to see if you can find his family. Can you do it without raising the suspicion of the department?"

"It's mighty risky right now. It might give us a lead, but it might also enrage his family, if he has one."

"See what you can do. Until Bob reappears, dead or alive, I don't know which way to jump." I paused. "By the way, Anna will have some lab results by early next week. I'll keep you apprised. Maybe that will give us some direction."

"That's good news. We can't sit around and wait for something worse to happen. Remember, no matter what, this isn't our fault.

These people were dead or involved before we came on the scene."

"But we are responsible for saving ourselves. I want you to promise me that we'll work together, and not against each other."

Roy nodded.

"Good, let's eat. It looks great. I'll never be able to give up fried food, it tastes so damn good."

Roy licked his lips. I was momentarily distracted. "It is a nice restaurant. You've always had great taste in restaurants." As I gazed out the window, I saw an alligator surface. But an animal predator here and there never bothered me. It's the human ones that are unnerving.

"Thanks. That's all I've heard, and it's fairly hush-hush. How about you?"

"Anna and I have determined where the nine millimeter we found at the beach ties in. We think we have anyway."

"How?"

"We checked the evidence vault and found the Jeffries case. The firearm and the shells we dug up at the beach belong to the lab and to the Jeffries case. It was evidence submitted in the first trial. But, there is a matter of the missing evidence from the first trial, namely shoes with bloody soles and some fingerprint evidence. The shoes and fingerprint evidence disappeared before the first trial. Only we didn't know this until recently."

"Why would Bob bury the gun and bullets at the beach?"

I ignored his question.

"You realize that we have another nine millimeter to contend with."

"What do you mean?"

"Anna found another one at Belle. It was buried in the well outside the house, so at this point we don't know which one killed Wayne—the one in the well or the one buried in the sand. Both guns will have to be tested."

"So, there's an extra gun. That means there may be another dead body out there somewhere."

"Maybe, maybe not. One could have been used to kill Wayne, and one to kill Billy Shipley. Or none of the above."

"But it's fair to say that at least one of them killed Wayne, right?"

"Only Bob can tell us that. He may have destroyed the original nine millimeter semi-automatic that killed Wayne. He may be planting guns everywhere hoping to confuse the feds."

"If the feds are hoping to reopen the case, they will have a hard time if the evidence is tainted."

"Is that what you heard, Roy? That they're here to reopen the case? Are those nuts going to be exhuming bodies from A to Z?"

"I heard that through the grapevine. Don't repeat it. They're looking into some kind of high-level official misconduct."

"Share all your information, Roy. Don't divulge it in little bits and pieces."

"I didn't know it was important. I'm sorry."

"From now on, just tell me everything you find out, regardless of which law enforcement agency it relates to."

"I will."

"It's all right. I'm more than a little touchy when it comes to the FBI."

"I know. None of us like them, dear."

"Don't call me that. It sounds like I'm an animal or something—and it's more than being a little touchy about the FBI. I truly believe that they are following me, breaking into my house and Anna's house, and bugging our phones. Have you checked your own phones?"

"Well, no. What do you mean following you?"

"They followed Jean and me out of town last weekend, or I believe it was them. I tried to call you about it, but you were out on a big drug bust. Yesterday, someone broke into Anna's house, and when I returned home from the office, I found a man in a ski mask in my house. I should have called the police when I couldn't find you. My phone and Anna's attic were both bugged, and we have the evidence to prove it. Who but the FBI would have access to that kind of wiretapping equipment?"

"Now, who's been holding out information?"

"Yes, but that's all of it. It's hard to trust you, Roy."

"The answer to your question is that very wealthy crooks have access to the same equipment the FBI does. You don't know who or what you're dealing with, Micki. Proceed with caution, wherever you go, whatever you do."

With that last comment, Roy fell silent. We had finished our meal, and he requested the check. I wondered if he was waiting for me to pick up the check or pay my part. He was a notorious cheapskate. To my surprise, he paid it. Jean would've been proud of him.

"Thank you, Roy, for both the lovely lunch and the information. I'll be out of town after today for a long weekend, but I'll be back on Monday. If anything is discovered while I'm away, I want to be notified first thing Monday morning, at my home or office."

"Going to see hubby?"

"That's right."

"Have a good time, because when you get back, we're all in for the ride of our lives."

"I don't mind the ride, it's the rap I'm not willing to take. Roy, do me a favor and go see Anna. No phones. Tell her everything you told me. I'd do it, but there isn't time. When I get back to my office, clients will be waiting and then Sherry is dropping me off at the airport."

"It's as good as done. I'll meet Anna for dinner tonight somewhere quiet. Just think, two pretty ladies in one day. How lucky can a guy get?"

"Two pretty married ladies. Don't get carried away."

"I'm not. We'll all survive."

"I hope you're right."

Roy walked me to my car. There were no sexual overtones today, no sexual tension either (except the lip licking). Must be my familial state of mind looking forward to the trip. I arrived back at the office just minutes before Meyers showed up. I pulled his file and pretrial motions to review with him. I'd rehearsed the lecture I was going to give him about skipping out on me for weeks at a time.

"Sherry, send Mr. Meyers back, please."

As he strolled in I notice his tight black leather pants and matching mesh tank top. I ignored his cruising apparel and got down to business.

"Hi, Mike, where've you been?"

"Oh, you wouldn't believe it." He was gesticulating.

"No, I probably wouldn't, so just skip the bullshit."

"You're mad at me?" he asked in a hurt voice.

"Damn right, I'm mad. You made me look like a fool in front of Judge Carroll a few days ago. You had a court appearance, and you didn't show. I was there, but you weren't. The case was reset, and I informed the judge that if you disappeared on me again that I was withdrawing. You got that?"

"I got it, but I have a good excuse."

"There is no good excuse, unless you were dead or dying. You need to learn how to use a telephone."

"I understand. It won't happen again."

"You're right. It won't happen again, not to me anyway. It might happen to your next attorney."

"I don't want another attorney."

"And believe me, no other attorney wants you either. Lawyers don't like representing child molesters, but the judicial system requires us to defend people like you who fondle undercover cops and molest children. With your criminal history, if you think a jury is going to cut you any slack, you're sadly mistaken. Who's going to believe that you were blowing on your seven-year-old nephew's belly like you would a baby, and suddenly he rears up and his dick is in your mouth?

"You go ahead and tell that story and see if the jury sends you straight to the penitentiary for life. They'll be looking for any reason to send you away. Your behavior is sick, and you need more than legal help. If you don't sign up for the classes we spoke about, then I'll withdraw as your lawyer. If you don't see a therapist," I reiterated for emphasis, "I will not represent you. You have four days to do as I've instructed. Come Monday, if you haven't contacted a therapist, then I will no longer be your attorney, understood?"

"Yes." He was subdued.

He looked down at the floor. I felt bad about my outburst, but we had discussed parameters before I agreed to take his case. Sometimes it was hard to be firm with clients, even when they deserved it.

"Good. Now, let's review your pretrial motions."

Mr. Meyers left the office quickly after we reviewed his

motions. Afraid of a closing lecture, I'm sure.

Only one more case, the Hines divorce. I arranged to see her in the conference room.

Mrs. Hines and I reviewed her discovery, which was due early next week. Sherry had been working on it for several days now. We had been through two depositions, propounded and responded to interrogatories, requests for production, and admissions. Simply put, we had sent the other side, the cheating husband, many sets of questions and requested lots of documents. In response, they asked for as much information. There was so much paper, I'm certain between the two sides we had killed a couple of redwood trees.

Once my clients were gone, I collected my suitcase from the car and placed it in Sherry's Isuzu. "Let's go, girl. You get to leave an hour early today."

Sherry drove like a wild woman all the way to the airport. I finally spoke up.

"Hey, I'm not in a hurry. The plane doesn't leave for two hours."

"I'm sorry. It always makes me nervous when I get near an airport. I've had some near misses and bad experiences."

"That's weird. I never see you get nervous about anything."

"Oh, I have my moments, but I put on a brave face for you."

"I appreciate that."

She screeched up to the curb. I thanked her, took out my suitcase, checked in, and got my boarding pass.

Chapter Nineteen

I sat down at the gate with the others awaiting our flight to Denver. Retrieving the transcript from my briefcase, I began to read to pass the time. Unable to concentrate, I found myself people-watching: babies crawling around on the dirty airport floor, mothers chasing them, tanned young couples returning from tropical paradises, businessmen and women coming and going, honeymooners headed for exotic locations. I sat mindlessly and watched these people, and missed my loved ones. It was a relief to get away for a while. I needed to be with Les and Michael.

I looked up and everyone was boarding. I never heard the announcement. I picked up my bag and got in line. The flight would be short enough, about two hours. I sat down next to a guy who already had his nose in a laptop computer. Oh well, he wouldn't be chatting in my ear the whole flight. I'd be able to skim most of the Jeffries transcript, and finish up on the flight back. I ignored all the safety ramblings of the stewards and pulled out the transcript again. It wasn't very long because the trial ended before rebuttals. I began flipping through pages to the place where I left off last night, before I fell asleep. Oddly enough, Jake Edmonds testified in his own behalf. His testimony was quite interesting where he touched on a potential motive.

The District Attorney, Mack Nobles, didn't fully explore this. A mistrial was declared toward the end of the defendant's testimony. The DA never got the opportunity to question Jake Edmonds regarding his motive to murder Wayne Jeffries. First the DA called Jake a liar, referred to him as crazy, alleged facts not in evidence, alluded to a prior jail sentence, and basically had a pissing contest with the defendant. The defense attorney was smart enough to allow this to continue for awhile, and then he seized his opportunity and requested a mistrial, which was in fact granted by Judge Herman. The interesting part of Jake's testimony read as follows:

The District Attorney (Mack Nobles): "Mr. Edmonds, what was your relationship with the deceased?"

Jake Edmonds: "I worked for him, up until the day he died."

DA: "You mean since he died, you are no longer employed by his company?"

JE: "No, I mean he fired me the day he was killed."

DA: "I see. What time of day did he fire you?"

JE: "In the evening. I had come back from distributing coffee and condiments about six."

DA: "So your duties with this company were distributing coffee and condiments?"

JE: "Yeah, and tea, cocoa, and snacks."

DA: "Who did you deliver to?"

JE: "Oh, lots of companies, homes in the west end of town, lots of businesses and restaurants."

DA: "Why were you fired?"

JE: "Well, Mr. Jeffries said that there had been some complaints."

DA: "What kind of complaints?"

JE: "Mr. Jeffries accused me of stealing from rich people in the west end of town."

DA: "Did you steal from them?"

JE: "No, sir, I'm not a thief."

DA: "But you had access to the homes of some of the wealthiest people in town, didn't you?"

JE: "Yes, I've been in and out of their homes for years. It don't mean I stole from them."

DA: "You could have had keys to their homes made during all those years, couldn't you?"

JE: "I wouldn't do that."

DA: "Why not? It's tempting for a guy like you, isn't it?"

JE: "What do you mean by that?"

DA: "I mean a cold-blooded killer and liar, like yourself. It would have been easy."

JE: "I never killed nobody."

DA: "Sure, you did. Your fingerprints were found all over the deceased's home."

JE: "Well, I've been to his house lots of times."

DA: "Your bloody shoe-prints were discovered by the desk, where you shot him in the back, the desk he tried to dive under to save his own life." (Shoes that never made it to trial.)

JE: "I didn't shoot him. I already told you that."

DA: "Tell the truth, you lying piece of scum. Prison made you an even bigger liar, didn't it?"

Defense Attorney William Nevers: "Objection. Your honor, this has gone on long enough."

Judge Herman: "Too long, counselor."

That big hint gave the defense attorney his way out, and he took it.

Defense Attorney William Nevers: "Judge, the defense requests a mistrial. The State has accused the defendant of being a liar, a murderer, and scum in the presence of the jury, and it serves to prejudice the jury to the extent that they would be unable to render a fair and impartial verdict in this case."

Judge Herman: "Your motion is granted."

Too bad the State never got the chance to ask the really important questions about Jake's relationship with Wayne Jeffries. The suspect had a motive, one that had never come to light in the press, or with law enforcement for that matter. They were off on other bunny trails, and they didn't investigate Jake's being fired—or did they? How could they have failed to discover that Jake had sticky fingers?

Wayne made one simple mistake, and that was confronting Jake. Jake must have been tied to an underground of criminals, or else he would never have walked away without a prison sen-

tence for murdering his friend and employer of fifteen years. It
didn't make any sense unless there were others involved in the
cover-up. The DA mentioned bloody shoe-prints during the trial,
but never referred to the shoes themselves. Where were they?

"Please fasten your seatbelts. We are approaching Denver
and will be landing momentarily."

The pilot broke into my reverie. I put the transcript back in
its folder and then concealed it in a leather zipper case. I didn't
want Les to see it, and I'd try not to think about it too much until
I left Colorado. That would take great effort. I had to call Roy
and have him investigate the burglary allegations against Jake.
Maybe tonight I could slip away and make that call.

After about twenty minutes, we were on the ground. I pushed
through the crowd. I was anxious to see my husband and son.
They had the most wonderful smiles on their faces, Michael was
running toward me.

"Mamma, Mamma. Over here."

I scooped him up in my arms, he felt so good.

"I missed you, Michael."

"I missed you, too, Mamma."

Les made his way past the crowd. He was tall and thin with
hair the color of chestnuts, and his walk always caught my eye.
He moved toward us and embraced Michael and me. It was fan-
tastic, the three of us together again. A three-way hug, my
favorite hug of all.

We had a long walk to the car so I made a stop by the ladies'
room before exiting the airport. My mind wandered back to the
transcript. I had to call Roy now or I'd obsess about Jake's burglaries throughout the entire trip. I hated talking about it over the
phone, but that couldn't be helped. Surely the feds wouldn't have
infiltrated the police department. But Roy wasn't at work. I did-
n't have his unlisted home phone number. So I called Anna at the
lab. I used our old code. Two rings, hang up, call again.

"Is that you?"

"It's me."

"I thought you'd be in Denver by now."

"I am, but something came up, and I needed to reach Roy."

"He's out on a bust. He called earlier and put me on notice. I may be needed later as well. I told him to handle matters himself if he could, because I'm swamped here. It's only a small drug bust anyway."

"Are you having dinner with him tonight?"

"Yeah. He called after lunch and said you suggested it. What's up?"

"Well, I was reading the trial transcript on the plane this afternoon. Something interesting in the defendant's testimony never came up after the mistrial. I realize the police and prosecutors don't tell us much about the testimony prior to or subsequent to our involvement in any case. We focus on the forensics, and if it doesn't deal with science applied to the law, then the prosecutors don't discuss it with us. Anyway, Jake was stealing from Wayne's customers. When Jake testified, the District Attorney asked him specifically why Wayne fired him, and he said that it was due to allegations of theft. See, Wayne confronted him about the thefts, and Jake denied everything. He shot him in the back, so Wayne's accusations must have had some merit. My question is, why didn't anyone follow up on this after the mistrial? The District Attorney knew about the burglaries prior to trial, because he questioned Jake about them on the witness stand."

"They're hiding something, huh?"

"Big time. It's imperative that Roy find out why the DA covered up the issue regarding the burglaries after the trial. Jake was never prosecuted for them. Tell Roy all about it tonight. Tell him to be careful. It looks like we have some bigger fish to fry. Office clean?"

"Clean."

"I have to go now. Be careful, but get Roy motivated."

"I will. Have a good trip."

I left the restroom quickly.

"Thought you fell in," Les teased.

"No. Just a long line in the ladies' room."

Les had the four-day itinerary planned, complete with our first stop; Ouray, a wonderful alpine village surrounded by towering mountains. Victorian shops, gourmet restaurants, and quaint motels lined the downtown streets. Michael would love Box Canyon Falls, which featured a plummeting waterfall in a deep canyon. We would visit the historic hot spring pools, and drive our jeep on the unpaved roads leading to abandoned gold and silver mines. We were staying at a bed and breakfast for three nights. Then on to Owl Creek Pass on Saturday, where the trout fishing would be a dream.

Michael slept as we drove. He was missing the Million Dollar Highway, but Les told me Michael got up early and had been excited all day. Foolishly, I had been afraid he would forget about me and think I was just some voice over the phone. Les asked about my practice, and I asked how his building project was progressing. We told each other the latest jokes and laughed a lot. Once we arrived in Ouray, Les carried Michael to the room and we tucked him in together.

It was after eleven when Les went out to get us something to eat. I unpacked a few things and took a hot bath while he was gone. It was a chilly evening, and I pulled out Les's warm terry-cloth robe and wrapped up in it. Michael looked like a little angel. When Les returned I was watching him sleep.

"He's so beautiful, isn't he?" I said. Les nodded, and put his arm around my shoulder. We stood there for a few minutes.

All of the restaurants were closed, but the Bed and Breakfast had improvised and done a splendid job of providing us a meal of tasty morsels. Then we lay in bed and looked at the onyx sky outside our window. The stars virtually danced and shone with delicate bursts of light. We held each other for awhile. It was such a relief just to be together again.

"I can't bear the thought of leaving Sunday without you and Michael. I don't know how much longer I can stand the separation."

"Why don't you take him home with you? He's spent enough time in Colorado, and I think he misses his home and his mommy."

"What about you?"

"I'll be home next weekend for the reunion, and I expect to finish up here within a few weeks. It won't be much longer."

I felt much better knowing all this would end soon—both the separation from my family and the current ordeal Roy, Anna, and I were involved in. This was all coming to a head, I could feel it in my bones. Too much time had already elapsed, and it was time for the fat lady to sing. Funny, but some things I could feel and foresee so clearly for other people. But with matters that involved me directly, the issues were muddier. It was never a bright line case.

It had been a long, tiring day so we grownups were asleep before midnight. At three Michael woke up and didn't realize where he was. We comforted him, and he went back to sleep. We were wide awake. We took advantage of the moment and had a quickie. It had been weeks since we'd made love, and it was over in a heartbeat for both of us. It was tired, comforting sex, just a temporary fix until we both had more energy. It reminded me of the all-nighter sex we had the first few years of marriage. Back then we couldn't get enough of each other.

Morning came quickly, and after a lovely breakfast with the proprietors of the Spangler Inn, we left to explore our favorite Colorado village. After showing Michael Box Canyon Falls, we explored a few antique shops and went backpacking. Then we rented some bicycles and drove to Ridgeway, a historic old town with a fine mountain bike trail system. We finished up the afternoon mountain biking. Michael sat behind Les and loved every mile of it. As it was getting dark, we started back to Ouray to finish the day with a dip in the hot springs and dinner at the Pinion Restaurant.

"Have fun today?" Les asked.

"I had a great time."

"What would you like to do tomorrow?" he asked.

Les and I were both compulsive when we traveled. We squeezed in as much as we possibly could every day. It would have been out of character for either of us to sit back, relax, and take it easy.

Friday morning we got up, ate a hearty breakfast, packed our jeep for the day, and departed for Imogene Pass over to Telluride. Driving over the mountains the tree lines were well below us. In Telluride, we had a picnic lunch at a small park. Michael played on the swings.

After lunch we drove back to Ouray. Les had been to Colorado every summer since he was a teenager. It was his favorite state, and it had all the things he loved: the mountains, snow skiing, backpacking, bicycling, and hunting. On the other hand, I leaned more toward the beaches: Hawaii, the Bahamas, Puerto Vallarta, and the Virgin Islands. I was crazy about scuba diving, snorkeling, water skiing, beach combing, and water sports in general. We had different upbringings. The swamps made me yearn for beautiful, white, sandy beaches and emerald water. Les grew up in the panhandle, close to Colorado, and he loved the mountains with their icy trout streams. We stopped at a park on the return trip to Ouray and let Michael stretch his legs and run around.

"Mamma, look!" Michael had ducks all around him.

"They like the bread you're feeding them, don't they?"

"But they won't go away." Michael seemed a little scared.

"They aren't going anywhere until you feed them every last bite of bread," Les told him.

"What kind of duck is this, Daddy?"

"It's a mallard, a greenhead. He's the daddy duck."

"Which one is the mamma duck?"

"She's called a hen, and she's the brown one."

"Why are they different colors?"

"So the daddy duck can attract the attention of the mamma duck. Then when the mamma duck is going to have the baby ducklings, she won't attract as much attention because she doesn't have that bright green head. She can hide from other animals that might hurt her and the baby ducklings."

Michael seemed to like that explanation. I figured the next question would be how the mamma ducks have the baby ducklings, but I guess he's a little young for those kinds of questions, and I was relieved. A five-year-old is more than capable of unanswerable philosophical questions.

The drive back to Ouray made me long to be a painter or photographer. When the evening sun glittered across the mountain tops and shimmered upon the lakes, it lit up the quaking aspen trees. Everything took on an ethereal quality.

I had no bad dreams here, no fear of being stalked, followed, or harassed. I hadn't even thought about the case in two days. What a miracle. I wasn't going to slip back into that darkness now.

Les seemed to sense my darkening mood. "What are you

thinking about, sweetheart?"

"Just how beautiful everything is, and how much I'll hate leaving on Sunday."

"Too bad we can't stay for a month, isn't it?"

"It's too bad that our lives and our jobs won't permit it."

"Someday we'll retire and we can stay here for months at a time."

"That seems a long way off." I sighed.

Michael had dozed off. A nap would do him good, because he always exhausted himself on these trips. Les had his arm around me, and we sat close and talked about the future most of the drive back to our bed and breakfast. We picked up our swimsuits and Michael awakened before we reached the springs.

"Are we going swimming now?" Michael asked.

"Right now," I answered.

"Did I go to sleep long?"

"You didn't miss anything. We wouldn't let that happen." I smiled at my energetic son. He never stopped moving. He was so full of life and always in motion, like me. Like his father, he loved being out discovering new places.

The springs had different levels of heat, from lukewarm to a piping 105 degrees Fahrenheit. You could move from one area to another once you were accustomed to the warmth of the water. Michael liked to swim around in the cooler parts. With Michael several yards away, Les and I were able to caress each other under the water. It felt good. After relaxing for a while, we returned to the room to dress for dinner.

Michael fell asleep in our booth after he ate. We carried him to the jeep and then back to the room. We talked for a while and then packed for Owl Creek. Michael would be so excited tomorrow when he learned that we were going fishing.

Rather than camp out, we opted for a cute cabin in the area near the Silverjack Reservoir. Early spring in the mountains, it was still fairly cold. It was Saturday morning, and Michael was awake before sunrise. His fishing gear was laid out, and he was inspecting it.

"We are going fishing today?" he asked.

"It's today." Les and I responded. We laughed.

"Oh, boy, I hope I catch the biggest one."

"I'm sure you will," I told him.

"What day is today, Mamma?"

"Saturday. Why?"

"How many more days do we have?"

"Two—today and tomorrow."

"I wish we didn't have to leave."

"So do your father and I."

"When do you go home, Mamma?"

"Sunday. Would you like to come home with me?"

I had decided to leave him with my folks when he wasn't in school.

That way I knew he'd be safe.

"That would be good. Is Daddy coming too?"

"Not yet, but soon—and he'll be home next weekend for the family reunion."

"But first I want to go fishing."

"Come on gang, let's go. Owl Creek Pass awaits us." Les was in a hurry to get going.

There was another reason we had taken a cabin. We wanted some privacy. Les and I needed to be alone for a few hours. The sexual tension was killing us both. I found myself touching him every chance I got. He couldn't keep his hands off me either. We were more than ready to "do it."

During the scenic drive, each of us was mesmerized by the beauty of this part of the country. Once we reached Cimmarron Road it was a rocky ride. Then it was on to Silver Jack Reservoir and Silver Jack Campground. The drive offered spectacular views of Courthouse Mountain and Chimney Rock. We would be staying in a cabin near the reservoir in the Uncompahgre National Forest.

Finally, we arrived at our cabin, and got the key from the owners, a sweet old couple that we met several years ago on our first stay at the cabins. Margaret and Kyle Stewart had lived in Minnesota until they retired. After fighting mud slides and snow practically year round, they moved to Colorado and invested in some cabins near the Silver Jack Reservoir. We always enjoyed seeing them.

"Margaret, the Lanes are here." Kyle was smiling and wearing the very same fishing cap he wore the first time I met him.

"Hello, hello," she greeted.

Margaret had a round figure and sweet disposition.

"My, haven't we grown," she beamed at Michael.

"We're going fishing," he told her.

"Well, you be sure and catch a big one. You won't have to buy your supper if you catch a big enough one."

"Can we cook them over a fire, Daddy?"

"If we catch enough, we can."

"What do you need besides the key? I've got fresh apple pie."

"We'll take a quart of milk, that apple pie, and the key." Les rubbed his stomach.

"Be sure to come up for breakfast in the morning, Margaret is still cooking her famous breakfasts. We don't even use a menu anymore, she does it all," Kyle boasted. Margaret blushed.

The men discussed bait for a minute, then I grabbed the key and off we went. Our cabin was next to a small pond. The mountains were in the background, and there was a hearty stand of aspen trees near our front door. The cabin had a kitchen, a small bath, two bedrooms, and a living area with a cozy fireplace. We would definitely need a fireplace tonight. The mountain air was much colder here than in Ouray, and I thought the temperature was dropping. We plopped our luggage on the beds, clutched our rods and reels, and walked toward our favorite stream. The trout were waiting.

About thirty minutes later, Les caught the first trout.

"Look at this," he shouted.

It was a nice rainbow trout. Stream trout were not as large as brown trout, but just as tasty.

"Daddy, Daddy, help me catch one. Please, Daddy."

"Okay, son. Let me get this one in the net and safely to shore, and then we'll catch one together."

Michael, Les, and I fished for a couple of hours. Michael caught several and was almost hysterical bringing in every one of them. I caught one, the biggest.

"Son, let's clean these now," Les told him.

"We going to eat these for supper, Daddy?"

"Yes, we are. We're going to get some potatoes and corn to go with them. And we'll have apple pie for dessert. How does that sound?"

"Good, I'm already hungry."

Les fried the fish outside over an open fire. Michael never left his side. He loved outdoor cooking. We sat down to eat by the campfire on a blanket, and Michael was impressed by this as well.

"How's your fish, son?" Les asked him.

"Really good, Dad, is this one mine?"

"Yes, I tagged him for you so you would get to eat the biggest fish you caught, and if you finish that one, here's another one for you."

The three of us ate, and then Michael took his bath. He lay in front of the fire Les built and went to sleep on his blanket. He was sleeping peacefully when Les carried him to bed. We removed the luggage from our bed and took a bath together, like we did in the early days of our courtship, before Michael. With the door locked and the bathroom all steamed up, Les and I began making love, the kind that resulted from two days of understated foreplay. Our seductive dance was urgent, intense, and provocative.

We couldn't help ourselves. But for the quickie, it had been weeks since we had been together. With Michael along, there hadn't been an opportunity until now to fully explore one another's bodies. At first, it was just kissing, then more tongue, deeper and deeper we pressed. Our bodies were slippery with soap and water as they moved against each other. Les began to kiss my breasts, then lick my nipples and nuzzle my neck with his nose. I carefully slid down to take him into my mouth. He moved against me over and over again. Then pulling me up to his mouth, he kissed me with an urgency equal to my own. He had let the water run out of the bath tub. As it was draining, he moved down in the tub and pulled me on top of his face. He began licking me and I arched my back and held myself up with my arms on the tile ledge just above us. It felt so good. I came like a shock wave.

Just after my climax, Les grabbed a towel, dried me gently, dried himself, and carried me to bed. He entered me, and I rolled over on top of him and rode him until he shuddered. As I climbed off of him, I moved down his pelvis and kissed him gently. He was aroused once more, and carefully lifted me over his face, a position we both liked. He had a long sensuous tongue, and lips that kissed and caressed in all the best places. After I could take no more, I lowered myself onto him once again and it began all over. I surrendered to my pleasure in the unique smell and feel of him.

We never spoke much during lovemaking, instead using our bodies for direction and affirmation. We had learned in our relationship that a touch, a sigh, a movement, a strategically placed tongue or lips, breast, or penis—did the trick for both of us. I felt free to let go and explore when Les and I had sex. My only responsibility was to please him. It was no less than sheer ecstacy. We made love until morning. We would be tired, but neither of us cared.

"Les, we can't wait this long anymore. It makes us crazy."

"It was a good crazy. Any cuts or bruises?"

"I don't think so. But a larger tub will be in order next time."

"A Jacuzzi or hot tub, at least."

The sun was up, and in a couple of hours, Michael would be awake.

"Better shut your eyes for awhile," I told him. "Our son will be up soon, and then the work begins."

"I'm glad he's going home with you. He's missed you, and I think you need him too."

"With all my heart, I need him. It will help the time pass until you come home."

"Soon, it will be soon," he said.

Michael woke up starving. The cold mountain air must have made him ravenous. We loaded up in the car and headed to the Stewart's for Margaret's famous breakfast.

"Good morning, folks. What can we get you?" Margaret greeted us.

"Michael would like some blueberry pancakes, an order of bacon, and a glass of milk. Les and I will have your smorgasbord and coffee."

"A little hungry this morning, are we? Coming right up." She grinned. Something told us she sensed a passion hangover.

"Hungry doesn't begin to describe it." Les whispered in my ear teasingly.

"Not hardly," I said.

We all ate heartily. Once we were sated, we paid the bill and our respects, and left for our last morning of the trip. We had planned to fish this morning then take one more look at Ouray on our way back to Denver.

Fishing was productive, and Les promised Michael that he would bring all the fish with him when he came home for my family reunion. I shot some panoramic pictures and video of the mountains, the trout streams, the aspen trees, and Michael and Les. I didn't do much fishing, I enjoyed watching them together. Michael gathered some colorful rocks from the streams to carry home with him. He had a rock fetish, and he usually carried one or two around in his pockets. I found them everywhere — all over the house, in the washing machine, his closet. Everywhere.

We ate a picnic lunch near a small bridge where we had fished the previous day. When we finished we returned to the cabin to pack for the drive to the airport. In Ouray we stopped at a glass-works boutique. We made a habit of bringing something special back for our home from each of our trips. This time we selected a piece of art glass, a heavy blown-glass vase. Its bright colors would remind us of the mountains, the aspen trees, the wild flowers, and all the beauty we had the privilege to behold for a few short days.

As we got nearer the airport, we all fell silent. None of us were ready to separate again. But, here we were at Stapleton Airport, and it was time for Michael and me to leave. I hated leaving Les, but at least I could take my boy home. Maybe that would help settle my nerves. The flight was short, and Michael napped on the plane. When we arrived at the local municipal airport, we took a cab back to my car at the office and went directly home.

Chapter Twenty

When we got home, Jorge was delighted to see Michael, and Michael talked to him like he was a sibling rather than a cat. Then Michael went to take his bath and went to bed. I told him I'd take him to his grandparents tomorrow after pre-kindergarten. While he was bathing, I went through the mail and stacked it in my briefcase.

The message center on my machine said I had three messages. One was from Jean, one from Anna, and one from Mom. I called Mom back first.

"Mom, I'm back."

"How was your trip?"

"Wonderful, too short. But I brought Michael back with me. It's been so lonely here."

"Bring him by tomorrow."

"I will, after school. By the way, can he stay with you and dad in the afternoons for the next few weeks? I didn't make after-school arrangements for him because I thought he was going to stay with Les."

"We'd love to have him. Just bring him by after school, or I can pick him up. Is Les coming in for the reunion?"

"Yes, and the job will be completed sooner than he anticipated, so he should be back within the month."

"I know that will make you happy."

"It discombobulated me when they both left. I felt odd and abandoned. It's a silly thing for a grown woman to feel, but I felt it all the same."

"You must come visit when you feel that way. You've been a stranger lately."

"I'm sorry. There's a lot happening at the office, and I'm help-ing Anna on a case."

"You are?"

"I am, but I can't really talk about it."

"Is it dangerous?"

"It could be."

"You better be careful. You know how your father hates see-ing your name in the newspaper when those nasty cases hit."

"I don't think my name will appear in the paper. Everyone is holding their cards pretty close to their vests at the moment. You don't need to worry."

"I hope not, for everyone's sake. Micki, you left police work years ago. Why get involved in something clandestine again?"

"I wasn't a policeman, mom." I was never careless. She should know that.

"You know what I mean." She could still hurt my feelings and never realize it.

"I know what you mean, and it's under control," I lied. My tone was even in my attempt to disguise my defensiveness.

"Well, see you tomorrow. Sweet dreams." She could turn it on and off. Sweet dreams indeed.

"Mamma, Mamma," Michael called out to me. I helped him with his pajamas and read him a story. He was sound asleep in less than ten minutes. I'd call Jean tomorrow morning, but I had to call Anna tonight.

"You still awake?" I asked her.

"Wide awake, and I will be awake every night until this thing is over."

"Got any big news?"

"Another dead body, Micki. Number three this time, counting Wayne. I'll meet you for lunch tomorrow and tell you everything.

I haven't had time for a lunch break since you left, but tomorrow I'm taking one, regardless."

I got the hint. She wasn't talking over the phone. She suggested we meet for lunch at Guadalajara.

"I'll be there, noon sharp—and Anna, I brought Michael back with me."

"Good. How is the little guy?"

"Fine. He's asleep, something I haven't been able to do for weeks, except when I was in Colorado. I slept like a baby those few days."

"I nearly forgot to ask how your trip was."

"It was beautiful, and such a comfort to be with Les. I haven't told him everything. I don't know if I can explain why I'm so entrenched in this thing without alarming him. I haven't been able to figure it out myself."

"You're better off keeping your mouth shut for now. There's no need to involve him, and it may be dangerous for anyone else to know. I mean, after all, three people are dead."

"I'll keep quiet. I don't know who to trust."

"No one. Trust no one. It's just the three of us now."

"Did you talk to LeRoy?" I asked.

"I'll tell you everything tomorrow."

I decided to call Jean. I was all jazzed up after my conversation with Anna. Jean would be up, she was a night owl. Her phone rang several times before she answered.

"Jean, I'm back from Colorado."

"How was it?"

"Incredible, the anti-climate to this muggy swampland."

"I meant the absence-makes-the-heart-grow-fonder sex, but I'll settle for a weather report. Was it cold?"

"Pretty dry and cold, but the mountain air, the wild flowers, the aspen trees, the fishing—it was all worth it."

"How are the boys?"

"Great. I brought Michael back with me."

"When can I see him?"

"What about me? Didn't you miss me?"

"All right. When can I see you both?"

"In a few days, once we've settled in again. You can take us to dinner."

"It would be my pleasure. Micki, I need to talk to you about something." Her tone changed.

"You know the psychiatrist I work for?"

"What about him?"

"It's not about him, it's about something he told me today."

"Well, let's hear it."

"It seems that this woman that I've been counseling for quite awhile sought me out for reasons that didn't have anything to do with therapy."

"What do you mean?"

"He referred her to another counselor because he knew I had a conflict of interest. But she called me on her own."

"What conflict?"

"She dated Guy for a while during one of our split-ups. She's been telling me her abusive marriage has her so screwed up. On the other hand, she talks about this other man she met, and how sweet and supportive he is. She has been mind-fucking me for months. She told me everything about this new man—except who he was. She knew he was my boyfriend when she sought me out. She even told me he liked to stay up late and talk for hours after sex. So much for his claim that he can talk so easily because I'm such a good listener!"

"That's pretty scary."

"Are there any legal steps I should take?"

"I think you better talk to Dr. Singer about this."

"I have. I found out when Dr. Singer was reviewing our billing and insurance claims. Her name looked familiar to him, and he asked me about her. When I described her, that's when he told me. What do you think I should do? I need to refer her to another counselor, but I have to be careful how I terminate our counseling relationship. I have to maintain confidentiality and make sure the referral is appropriate. This shouldn't be a problem since we've reached the point in her therapy where we would begin termination anyway. I'm going to refer her to someone else for relaxation training."

"Have you told Guy about this?"

"Not about her being a client. I asked if he knew her. He said there wasn't anything serious between them. They dated a couple of times, that's all. He hasn't seen her since we got back together the last time—or so he wants me to believe."

"What made you certain Guy dated her?"

"I saw her name and phone number in his address book. He picked her up in a bar. Great, huh?"

"You're pretty upset by this, aren't you?"

"Majorly devastated. This woman took great pains to find out who I was, find my employer, call me, and seek my services, all in an effort to fuck with me. Obviously because of my connection to a man she had become obsessed with."

"I can't really think of any law she's broken. I know that doesn't make you feel any better. There's no statute against a crazy asshole. At least not yet."

She laughed at this. "There should be."

"I'm happy to see you haven't lot your sense of humor."

"But I have, and I'm giving up counseling for awhile. I'm feeling burned out.

"I'm going back to teaching, where I can see tangible results relatively quickly. I've already called the university and put them on notice that I'm available for the fall semester. I think I'll take some time off this summer and travel. No more wackos."

"At least you have options."

"I'm wondering if her actions are enough to support the only exception to confidentiality, the risk of harm to herself or others."

"Sounds to me like she's capable of hurting you."

"I'm sorry to hit you with this, Micki, on your first evening back. I don't have anyone else I can talk to about this. Guy and I just broke up again. I've been ambivalent about the relationship for some time, and this incident convinced me it was over."

"You can always call me. You know that."

"Maybe some day I'll think it's funny, but not at this moment."

"You think that maybe tragedy plus time can equal comedy?"

"Maybe, once my wounds have healed. Speaking of wounds, how is your mystery case going?"

"I really shouldn't talk to you about it. It might be dangerous, even deadly."

"Deadly?" She gasped. "What have you done?"

"I haven't done anything, but there are other people out there doing things that are leaving dead bodies and a wake of destruction."

"Just be careful, and get away from that shit."

"I wish I could. My house has been bugged and I've been followed. Remember? You were there."

"I thought I had problems with patients stalking me and strange women seeking my so-called help, but your situation sounds worse. Maybe you should consider leaving town for a while."

"I can't, not until this is settled."

"That sounds really scary."

"It keeps me awake at night."

"Will Michael be safe with you?"

"I think so, he'll be in school during the day and with my parents in the evenings. I think we'll be safe in the house at night. Roy has someone patrolling the neighborhood from eight at night until eight in the morning. He ordered me and Anna to trust no one but each other. If I don't talk to you for a few weeks, it's to protect you."

"Don't be silly. No one is going to bother me."

"How can we know that? I've had those anxiety dreams about you—and I could never live with myself if something happened to you."

"Okay. If you need anything, I'm always here. I'll call your mom over the next couple of weeks. She'll tell me if anything weird comes up."

"Sure, and it's really been comforting to have a qualified counselor to confide in."

"Likewise. Get some rest. That little boy of yours will be wound up like he's battery-operated by tomorrow morning. And, Micki, I'm proud of you."

I hung up and immediately showered. Public transportation always made me feel dirty. I'd shower again in the morning. I checked on Michael, and he was sleeping quietly. Not stirring a bit, and he looked like a little blond doll.

Morning came much too quickly, but I slept better than I expected. Maybe I was tired from the trip. Or maybe it was having Michael home again. I noticed something else since I returned home: I hadn't thought of Roy in days. I needed to keep my head on straight for the big showdown.

I woke Michael, fed him breakfast, helped him dress, brushed his hair and teeth, and turned on a video of *Chitty Chitty Bang Bang* for him while I showered and dressed. He yawned all the way to school, and I asked him if he felt all right.

"I guess so. But I still feel sleepy. What time will you pick me up, Mamma?"

"I'll be back at three, okay?"

"And I'm going to mawmaw and pawpaw's?"

"Yes, and I'll be there by seven o'clock to have dinner and pick you up. Have a good day, sweetheart. Let me know if you need to make up anything you missed while you were with your daddy. Bring me a note from your teacher."

"I will." He was gone, running up the stairs to Robert E. Lee Elementary School. I went to school here, and I liked the idea of him going here as well.

Chapter Twenty-One

When I got to the office, Sherry was waiting for me with a stack of files.

"Have a good trip?" she asked cheerfully.

"Yep. Refresh my memory. What do I have this morning?"

"You have pretrial matters on a couple of cases, nothing heavy duty, and don't forget Mrs. Hines' temporary order hearing."

"Good, I'm not in a heavy-duty frame of mind this morning."

"I'll handle the other clients for you today. I can transfer the phones to the answering service when I get covered up."

"Sounds great, I'll be at the courthouse most of the morning, and then I have a noon meeting. I'll be back in the office by two."

I gathered my files, looked at notes I jotted down prior to the trip, and refreshed my memory as to the issues of each case. After grabbing my *Family Code, Code of Criminal Procedure,* and *Penal Code,* I was off to the courthouse.

I waited my turn before the judge and spoke with each of my clients in the hall. Most of the pretrial motions were nonevidentiary and required only short rulings from the judge. My hearings, including Mrs. Hines', were completed by eleven-thirty. After running to the district clerk's office for a copy of an indictment in a criminal case and making a trip to the judge's office, I left.

Once back at the office I organized my files and paperwork, computer docketed my trial settings, and hoped that some of these cases resolved themselves without the necessity of a trial. If not, my calendar would be impossible for the next six months. I was out the door at eleven forty-five and entering the parking lot of Guadalajara Restaurant with five minutes to spare. Anna was there, she was always early.

"Hey, kid." She always referred to me that way.

"Hi, beautiful." My usual response to her greeting.

We both ordered huge platters of Mexican food and a pitcher of tea. While we were waiting, I couldn't stand the suspense any longer, and I interrupted Anna as she munched on some tortilla chips.

"Let's have it. Who's the other dead body? There's Wayne, Billy—now who?"

"You won't believe it. That murdering, lying, cheating, poor excuse for a human being—Jake Edmonds—was found dead at the beach near Bob's cabin, of all places."

"Goddammit, after all this, that creep won't have to face another trial for killing Wayne. I was looking forward to seeing the look on his face when he was convicted and realized he'd rot in federal prison for the rest of his life."

"Shhh, not too loud. Someone may overhear us," Anna warned.

I looked around suspiciously. "I'm not good at this. All this hush-hush makes me nervous."

"Well, at least Jake got what he deserved."

"So, there is a much larger picture. If Jake murdered Wayne, then someone offed Jake to shut him up or contain his greed, or both."

"But who's behind all this?" Anna looked perplexed.

"Someone who knows a lot about the Jeffries case. Someone connected to law enforcement. They know too much not to have a connection. Anna, what if Roy is dirty?"

"You know Roy better than that. They cut Jake up with a chain saw or something, he was in a body bag of sorts when a dog dug him up at the beach. I don't know how long he had been there, the autopsy isn't complete yet. Roy would never be capable of that."

"Gross. Someone was making a statement, weren't they?" I felt a little guilty thinking Roy was part of the conspiracy.

"Yep. Cross us—and you'll get the same or worse."

"What an uplifting thought. I guess Bob is out as a suspect as well. He's too chicken-shit to be voluntarily involved in anything this dangerous. What else do you have?"

"Remember all those papers we found at Belle?"

"Yes, what about them?" Anna ignored my comment about Bob. She was still protective of him. I guess because she had been with him for so long. Or maybe because he had promoted her in a field that required a college degree, when she didn't have one.

She continued. "Roy came and picked them up. The FBI wants to look at them."

"Oh, great. Roy's holding out on us again. And conspiring with the FBI."

"Micki, I know for a fact that Wayne and Susan made several attempts at reconciliation before he died. As a matter of fact, the kids were with Wayne on spring break just before he was killed. Susan stayed in Dallas for a while after Wayne was murdered. I guess she didn't want to answer too many questions."

"She and Jake both had motive to kill him. She wanted his money, and Jake didn't want to go to prison for burglary. I wonder how big a part she played in Wayne's murder."

"Do you think she's involved?" Anna asked.

"Why else would she come back after living in Dallas for years? Who the hell wants to live here if they don't have family here?"

"I always thought she would divorce him in Dallas and never return. She hated it here."

"Did you know her well?"

"I knew Wayne for about ten years, but I never socialized with her. After she moved away Wayne was lonely, and he took me and Harry to dinner and the horse races once or twice."

"I'd love to know where she's hanging out these days."

"Get LeRoy to check that out for us."

"I will. I'm supposed to call him today."

"I bet he's sitting by the phone as we speak," she teased.

"Anna, I'm having some trouble being around him."

"Like hormone trouble?"

"Something like that. Slightly out of control urges. Unresolved feelings. That kind of stuff."

"And what do you plan to do about that?"

"I'm doing my best to ignore what I'm feeling, and maintain the status quo."

"Think you'll be able to do it?"

"I hope I've grown up enough to be in control of my own animal urges. Besides, sometimes I feel like I'm just trying to get even, show him what he missed by screwing me around. You know, payback."

"Some of us never grow up that way."

"I have all these little cubbyholes in my brain. I try so hard to keep them all sorted out, but when they begin to overlap, it's hard."

"You'll manage. You always do."

"I don't want to be strong, I want someone else to be strong for a change. Someone else needs to be responsible, loyal, trustworthy, dedicated, and all the other things I'm tired of being. I feel so tired lately. I want to sit back and let life happen and take it easy."

"You never take it easy. You are the most driven person I know."

"What a curse."

"By the way, I have all the DNA samples from Belle set up. It takes several days to clean up the samples enough to extract the DNA. Soon I'll have something to tell you. I've set up all the blood scrapings you collected from the trunk in the barn. I did the Ouchterlony testing to determine whether the samples were human blood, and they were. In three or four days, I should have DNA profiles for you."

"What do you have left to test from the crime scene, other than the blood?"

"Hairs, fibers, and other trace evidence that I will mount for microscopic evaluation, but if no comparison hairs or fibers come in, they won't mean much. Maybe we'll get something from

Jake's body, his car, his house, something to compare them to."

"The evidence found at Belle could be a hundred years old. Who knows? Any word on where Bob is?"

"Not yet. If he's alive I bet the news about Jake has him all a twitter. I don't get his connection to Jake in this deal, unless Bob was bought off. Where would Jake get enough money to pay off Bob? Wayne did leave Susan very well off. Maybe Susan bankrolled Jake to do her dirty work."

"I don't know. Maybe he delivered coffee and condiments–and absconded with jewelry."

"Sorry to cut this short, Micki, but I have to set up for the grand jury today. It's already one-thirty."

"I should get back as well. I need to run a few errands before I pick up Michael at school by three."

"Give him a hug for me, and call me tomorrow if you can."

I ran to the bank, the cleaners, and the grocery store. I couldn't get the nagging suspicion out of my head that maybe, just possibly, Roy was entangled more than he let on.

Michael wasn't waiting for me on the front steps. I walked all around the school looking for him. Oh, God, don't let anything happen to him. Where was he? He always stood on the steps and waited for me. It's my fault. Someone's grabbed him. Why did I bring him home? How could I put him in danger? What kind of selfish mother am I? I ran around the school again. I went in the back door and checked every classroom. Some teachers were gathered in the hallway. They hadn't seen him. Before they could offer to help I ran out the front door.

"Mamma, Mamma, I made something for you," he called as he ran up the sidewalk toward me.

"What do you have here?" I strained a smile and clutched him to my chest. "Michael, where were you? I was worried."

"It's a picture of me, you, and Daddy."

"We'll hang it on the refrigerator with the others." I didn't want him to see me shaking.

"Where were you?" I asked again.

"I was looking at the puppies. See?" He pointed toward a large pecan tree where several children were standing and holding puppies. I don't know how I missed him. I looked that direction, but panic must have blurred my vision.

When I dropped Michael off, I assured my folks that I would be there by seven. Then I ran by the house to drop off the groceries. On my way back to the office I called Roy. I was still a bit shaken up.

"Roy, it's Micki, I'm back. Any news?"

"Some. Meet me. Same place, at six."

"Is it safe?"

"I think so, but watch your back."

"I will."

By four o'clock, I wasn't in the mood to work. After all, I did accomplish a little in court this morning, and I met with Anna for lunch. No, no slacking. I better get back to the office. As I pulled into the garage of my office building, loneliness enveloped me. My husband was away, my son was with my parents, and I missed them.

Legal work could be a lonesome occupation. You're forced to work long hours day after day, night after night, and most of the effort was of a solitary nature. You couldn't concentrate in a room full of people, at a party, at a movie, or skiing down the river, so you missed a lot of things. You told yourself it was worth it, but was it really? You didn't get the time back, and no one was keeping track of how many butts you saved. My priorities were definitely changing, and when this ordeal with the lab was over, I would make some critical adjustments to my long-term plans.

"You back?" Sherry heard the back door to our office open.

"For awhile, but I'm not in the mood to be here today."

"I'll take the front line this afternoon, and you can be out of the office, researching, in court—whatever. Just tell me."

"What's on the agenda this afternoon?"

"Only one appointment. I'll reschedule it if you like."

"Who is it?"

"It's a new criminal case."

"When?"

"About thirty minutes. I didn't get much detail."

I sat at my desk and looked out the window. Mondays were tough. After organizing case files from this morning, I turned on my laptop computer to check my schedule. Not too bad, I thought. I might survive the week, even with my morose mood. Sherry knocked at my door.

"Micki, this is Mr. MacNamara, Bob MacNamara."

Jesus. The old scumbag, disappearing ex-boss was standing in my office. I gathered my wits before Sherry could notice my discomfort.

"Thank you. Please see to it that we are not disturbed."

"Sure, no problem." She gave me a concerned look.

Once the door was shut, he sat down in my favorite chair, a brightly covered antique in violet velvet. He lit a cigarette and looked up at me. I hadn't seen him for thirteen years. His hair was nearly white now, his complexion ruddy. Bloodshot blue eyes and broken capillaries in his nose made his drinking problem apparent to anyone who knew the signs of alcoholism. Still skinny as a rail, the wiry son of a bitch puffed away.

"Please don't do that in my office."

"Sorry. I'm kind of nervous."

"Why are you here?" I wasn't in any mood to be gracious.

"I'm in a lot of trouble."

"So I've heard."

"Roy told you?"

"I'll ask the questions, if you don't mind. It's my office."

"It's okay if he told you. I want you to be my lawyer."

"I can't be your lawyer, I despise you. Besides, there's a potential for conflict here. You have placed us all in grave danger, and for what? Greed?"

"I can explain, Micki."

"Don't bother, I don't want to hear a word, not one word. Roy thinks you're dead. Did you know that?"

"He does? Well, I'm not dead yet."

"You better talk to him. And find yourself another lawyer. It won't be me. I'm done representing people I hate the sight of."

"Why do you hate me?" He actually looked hurt.

"Take one minute to think about all the lousy things you did to me and Anna."

"I guess you're right, but can't you forgive me? And listen to what I have to say?"

"Absolutely not! Leave my office and — Bob, I'm calling Roy

to tell him you're not dead. You go see him. And take care of this so no one gets hurt."

"Please, I need to tell you about Belle. It will be confidential, won't it?"

"What do you mean 'confidential?'"

"I mean with everything that's happened in the bayou, I need to get some legal advice."

"Don't tell me about your bayou bullshit, I won't hear it. I know I've said 'no' at least three times by now."

He persisted. "But—but wouldn't anything I tell you be privileged?"

"Only if I'm your lawyer. I'm telling you for the last time. No, no, hell no. I won't be your lawyer. As a matter of fact, if I get the chance, I'll testify against you, you low-life jackass."

"The bayou is rich, and you can be a part of it if you'll only listen. Anyway, everything I tell you will be privileged, either because of your past fiduciary duty to the lab, or in your capacity as my lawyer."

"So your request is that I represent you in my past capacity as a forensic toxicologist and my present capacity as an attorney, which will ultimately bestow upon you some magical bayou privilege. I think not. Now get out."

I opened my door with such force that it banged the wall. Sherry jumped.

"Sherry, show Mr. McNamara out, please."

She got up from her desk and escorted Bob to the front door. He wasn't much taller than me, maybe five feet eight. I could probably whip his ass, so Roy wouldn't need to.

When she sat down again, I told her not to take his calls. She nodded.

I walked back into my office, closed the door, locked it, sat down in my chair, and picked up the phone. I paged Roy, and waited for him to call me back.

"Micki, you have a call. An Officer Roberts," Sherry notified me over the intercom.

"Bob came to see me."

"What did he want with you?"

"Wanted me to be his lawyer, and I said 'no way.'"

"Micki, you might think about it. It's one way to get him to talk. He may be the key to all this—and without him it could take us forever to figure out who the players are."

"There is an underlying potential for conflict of interest. First of all, your interests and Bob's may be a consideration, and what about me and Anna? Before all this is over, we may all have conflicting interests." My radar went off for a second. Jean had warned me not to trust Roy. I wondered if Roy sent Bob to set me up.

"I hope not." His tone was somber. "But are we still on for this evening?"

"Yes. I'll see you shortly."

"Did you bring Michael home with you?"

"Yes. And Roy, I don't want my son in any danger because of my connection to this case."

Roy got the message loud and clear. I did my obsessive-compulsive routine around the office, arranged my desk, pulled files for tomorrow, then left.

I sat in the stadium parking lot to wait for Roy. I was a little early. Roy drove up and parked beside me.

"A little brave today, are we?" I teased.

"What do you mean?" He had a puzzled look on his face.

"Parking beside me, instead of around the corner or the far end of the county."

"Oh that. I'm tired of looking over my shoulder."

"Me too. Have you heard from Bob yet?"

"Yes, he actually paged me right after you did, whining about how you wouldn't listen to him."

"What a creep. Why should I listen to him?"

"I told him you wouldn't represent him."

"What's he going to do?"

"I told him not to do anything until I talk to him again. He knows Jake is dead. That's why he's hiding out." It seemed that there had been a power shift since Jake was murdered. First Bob threatened Roy's kids. Now it appeared that Roy had the power, and he wasn't offering any explanations. I had a bad feeling.

"Where's he been?"

"He wouldn't say. And actually I don't care as long as he

doesn't disappear again before he tells me what's going on."

"Are you going to meet with him?"

"Yes. Tonight at the lab."

"Be careful. Don't put Anna in jeopardy."

"I'll wait until she's left for the evening."

"What have you found out since I was away?" I was curious.

"I did some checking on Billy Shipley. I sneaked into the sheriff's office and got his file. I found a letter of resignation. It seems that he was moving out of town to take another job. Then I pulled his original application to look for next of kin. He has a sister in Florida, so I called her. She said that Billy disappeared years ago, and she hasn't heard from him since. They were close, so she doesn't understand what happened to him. When she called the sheriff's office right after he disappeared, they told her he had taken another job and left town. But he never mentioned a new job to her.

"Then he transferred and Sheriff Harding told her that Billy's new job was in undercover work, so he wouldn't be able to tell her anything. She figured that Billy would contact her sooner or later, but he never did."

"Sounds like he got in the way, and they killed him."

"Yep, but I didn't have the heart to tell her. So someone very high up at the county is on the take, but what's the take? It must be pretty high stakes or they wouldn't take the risk."

"You better pump Bob for information. He's bound to know who killed Billy and Jake."

"I don't think Bob could actually kill anyone. He doesn't have the guts, but he may be indirectly pulling the trigger, if you know what I mean."

"Listen, Roy, I'm headed for my folk's house now, but I'll be home later. Let me know what you find out."

"I will."

As I drove away, I was thankful that I had gotten control of my feelings for Roy, at least for the present.

After dinner, I made my excuses and escaped home with Michael. It seemed more like home with Michael back. I wanted to call Les before it got late so Michael could talk to him before he went to sleep. They talked for a few minutes. Then Les and I made plans for me to pick him up at the airport when he came in for the reunion. After I put Michael to bed, I read for a while, then fell into a dreamless sleep.

Chapter Twenty-Two

We were up bright and early. I dropped Michael off at school with the promise that I would pick him up on time. Work seemed more appealing today than it did yesterday. I was over the Monday blues.

I checked in with Sherry, then walked over to the courthouse.

My digital phone rang on the way over. It was Roy. I didn't recall giving him my digital number. Later we would have a talk about that.

"Bob didn't show last night, but promised to meet me tonight. He was spooked for some reason. Said something about being watched."

"Call me tonight and debrief, Roy."

"You know I will."

"Got to go. I'm due in court this very minute."

"Talk to you tonight, counselor." I always hated it when he was sarcastic.

I entered the office of my favorite prosecutor. It was pitiful—old, with ugly metal furniture, cracked windows, and the smell of bat guano. Yuck. The courthouse had been infested with bats for years. Texans loved bats, because bats ate mosquitoes, grasshoppers, and locusts. Something about keeping an important ecological balance. Most Texans were so enamored with bats, they'd travel hundreds of miles to watch them come out of caves or caverns. During the nineties there was some discussion regarding making bats the state bird. There were definite rules and regulations controlling what you could do with problem bats. You could drive them away to another location, but you couldn't kill them.

"Good morning, Alan. What's going on?"

"Same old, same old. What do you need this morning?"

"The plea papers on Mr. Salazar and Ms. Boudreux."

"Here they are. Let's hope the judge doesn't bust the pleas. They're fairly light."

"Who's on the bench?"

"Hitler, the midget Nazi. Judge Peltier, of course." This particular judge was an asshole.

"Great." I winced. "Just what I need this morning. I don't have time for this crap today."

"None of us do, Micki."

"I know. Can't someone run against him in the next election?"

"No, but I heard a rumor that he might retire at the end of his term."

"Wouldn't that be a dream?" I rolled my eyes.

"As long as someone even less palatable doesn't get his position."

"This town is full of weirdos who would love his salary." Didn't I know it.

"Let's go, Micki. The judge will be calling the civil docket by now. He'll be all pissed off if we walk in after he's begun calling the criminal docket."

We entered the courtroom just in time to see the lady justice made of copper lying in state in back of the courtroom. It seems that she had fallen through the roof into the courtroom during a rain storm the night before.

Suddenly a bat swooped down over the head of one of the attorneys. He was dodging and swatting and cursing the bat when the judge said, "Mr. Lindsey, calm down. They only attack warm-blooded animals. And in your case, I don't think that'll be a problem."

The whole courtroom roared with laughter. Alan and I glanced back and forth from the reclining lady justice, over to the attorney under bat attack, and then back again at each other. We were hysterical. After a few minutes, the laughter subsided, and the judge returned to the serious business of calling the criminal docket. He reminded us that the lady justice would be removed at the end of the day and the roof would be repaired by Friday. My mood was giddy, and I was barely able to function for a few minutes. However, the tone changed as Judge Peltier rejected the first criminal plea of the morning.

"I won't accept this plea, Mr. Prosecutor. It is not appropriate under the circumstances."

"Your honor, what would be acceptable?" asked the chief prosecutor.

"It is not my job to determine that. It will be up to your office to set this case for trial or come up with an acceptable alternative."

The chief prosecutor looked over at Alan and shook his head. Alan peered over in my direction, and I knew what he was thinking. What would happen to his cases? Would his highness reject his carefully developed plea bargains or would he escape the humiliation?

My cases were called one after another. They passed muster with the judge. Thank goodness. I had been so distracted lately I feared that my clients would suffer for it. I returned to my office. The remainder of the day was uneventful, and I left early to pick Michael up from school.

Michael and I could spend some time together, and I wouldn't need to impose on my parents. We went swimming at the country club. It was a little early in the season, but Michael didn't seem to mind, because the pool was heated. Then we went home for the evening. Once Michael had his supper and a bath, he watched a Disney video, while I got ready for bed. The phone rang.

"Micki, it's Roy."

"What are we looking at?"

"Some pretty heavy stuff. Bob just told me that Susan hired Jake to kill Wayne for one and a half million dollars. The more than obvious motive is greed. Susan was the beneficiary of five insurance policies, which had face values of one and a half million dollars each. She acted like she wanted a reconciliation, and then played the part of the grieving widow, when all she really wanted was his money and her freedom."

"Where does Bob tie in?"

"I'm getting to that. Jake and Susan needed the evidence to disappear, so Jake could get off. Jake approached Bob. He had met Bob earlier at a downtown bar and knew that Bob had his demons. Jake and Wayne had previously discussed Bob's drinking problem, certain prostitutes, some drug action—that kind of thing. It seems that Wayne and Jake were also drinking buddies. A fact unknown to law enforcement at the time of trial. Jake blackmailed Bob with his past wrongdoings and bribed him with the promise of a lot of money. Jake promised not to reveal what he knew about Bob to the county commissioners and said he'd reward Bob with some of the insurance proceeds. It was up to Bob to make critical evidence secured by the crime lab disappear. Not too much, just enough to make the case circumstantial, just enough to set Jake free. And Bob cooperated. Remember the bloody shoes and fingerprint cards?"

"Yes. I remember Anna telling me that they were missing."

"Bob concealed Jake's bloody shoes and some fingerprints lifted at Wayne's house. Since there were no prints on the murder weapon, that meant no physical evidence to connect Jake to the murder. There was nothing to compare the bloody footprint to because nobody could come up with the shoes to prove it was Jake's."

"That's right. No eyewitnesses, no convincing physical evidence, and a dumb-ass for a prosecutor."

"So who killed Jake?"

"Bob doesn't know, but he's scared shitless. He's convinced that he's next."

"Bob was blackmailed and bribed to conceal evidence?" I couldn't believe it.

"The funny thing is, he hasn't gotten any money yet. Jake told him that Susan wouldn't disburse the insurance money till there was no possibility of a new trial. Jake said she wanted to be sure the mistrial would not become the pet project of any fledgling prosecutor."

"What would guarantee that?"

"I don't know. I think she and Jake were stalling."

"Bob stayed quiet all these years?" It was hard for me to believe that Bob hadn't babbled about Wayne's murder when he was drinking. Maybe he had better sense and self-control than I realized. Was it possible that Bob's alcohol and drug abuse problem wasn't as severe as I thought?

"What else could he do? He concealed evidence and had old skeletons in his own closet. They had enough to indict him, so he just waited and kept quiet."

"I still don't understand why Susan Jeffries would trust a crook like Jake Edmonds. He must have had some hold on her, other than the murder."

"Must have, but that's all I have right now."

"Did Anna leave the lab before the two of you met?"

"Yeah. I didn't see her car, and the lab was locked up when we got there."

"Keep me posted, Roy."

"Will do, and you do the same."

I sat for a minute or two, stunned by what I had just heard. Bob hid evidence for profit or because he was scared silly. It made me shiver to think he could be so low. I reached for the phone to call Anna and tell her what I had learned from Roy. She answered after the fourth ring.

"You busy?" I asked.

"No, I was just getting in. I was opening the door when you called."

"Anna, I talked to Roy."

"He must have called you right after he met with Bob. He's surfaced, you know. I was at the lab working late when I heard someone at the door, so I turned out the lights and hid in the vault until they left."

"Roy said he didn't see your car."

"While all of this is going on, I'm not using my assigned parking space."

"I guess you were upset when you heard about the blackmail scheme and the greed involved in Wayne's death."

"He deserved so much better. He had all that insurance so Susan and the kids would be well provided for if anything ever happened to him."

"Did you hear anything Roy isn't telling me?"

"One thing that's going to piss you off. Roy has been enlisted to sway you to represent Bob. Bob is certain that he'll be implicated in the retrial."

"What retrial? Jake's dead."

"Bob told Roy that the FBI is determined to find out who Susan's co-conspirator was."

"So who killed Jake and Billy Shipley? I'm sure it's probably one and the same."

"I don't know, and neither does Bob or Roy."

"I'd bet my life that Bob knows who killed them. It'll be a cold day in hell before I defend that bastard, and Roy knows it!"

"Bob said that he, and Susan, and Jake used to meet at the mansion. It was 'Belle this' and 'Belle that.' He's really obsessed with that place, and the bayou."

"I wonder what went on out there."

"Don't know yet, but a dead body and lots of bones, blood, and hair make the mansion an issue."

"What did Bob know about the dead guy from the sheriff's office?"

"Nada. Claimed he never heard of the guy."

"Somebody knew him."

"Bob's really upset about having to hide out. He had been spending most of his time at the mansion. That is, before both of the recent searches."

"Where did he get the money to support the mansion?" I asked.

"Inherited it, but he doesn't have enough left to keep it up. There are back taxes, insurance, the grounds to care for, maintenance, a bunch of problems he was telling Roy about. He wants the money to fix up his mansion and retire. That's about the size of it."

"Someone killed Jake, and Susan either did it or knows who did. Tell Roy to put some surveillance on her until he finds out who she's hanging out with."

"I'll tell him, and Micki?"

"Yeah."

"Don't tell Roy I overheard him and Bob. I don't trust anyone but you at this point."

"Don't worry."

I couldn't believe that Roy would try again to talk me into representing Bob. In his dreams. He knew I hated the bastard, and anyway how could I effectively cover his ass with Bob in the way?

I finessed Michael into bed and watched Jay Leno do his monologue. It was morning before I knew it. How wonderful. The insomnia seemed to be gone.

Chapter Twenty-Three

While I was on my way to work the next morning, I got a call on my digital phone. It was Jean.

"Micki, someone's trying to get into my house." I could hear the hysteria in her voice.

"Call the police."

"I did. They're too slow. Can you get Roy or somebody out here? I'm telling you this guy has a gun. I saw him running around the house with it."

"I'll call Roy. I'll be right there."

"Got your gun?"

"Yes. Why?"

"You may need it. I'm not leaving this house. Whoever it is will have to drag my cold, dead body out of it."

"Don't say that. Just hang on."

"They're breaking every window in the house, and I'm scared."

"Get somewhere safe—away from the windows and the glass. It sounds like they are just trying to scare you."

It took me just a few minutes to get there. When I arrived, I saw someone on the east side of the house. I couldn't tell if it was a man or a woman. It was someone small in stature, wearing jeans, a dark T-shirt, and a ridiculous black knit ski mask.

Broad fucking daylight. Who would be terrorizing someone in broad daylight? No one in their right mind.

That was it. It must be one of Jean's clients. My anxiety dreams about Jean must be related to her work, not mine. What a relief. Roy drove up as I was closing in on the intruder, my gun in hand.

I walked toward the east side of the house, where I could see the nut breaking the window with the butt of a revolver of some kind. I yelled out from a distance, "Get away from the house."

This idiot turned to face me and aimed the gun right at my head. Roy, who had been calling for backup on his patrol car radio, jumped the street curb, drove onto Jean's lawn, and leapt from his car. He positioned himself between me and the wacko.

"Drop it, motherfucker, or I'll blow your head off."

The ski-masked weirdo ran around the back of the house. Before we realized what was happening, he had fired a shot into a window. Jean screamed from inside, "Micki, I've been hit. I've been hit."

I couldn't believe it. How could she have been hit if she was hiding out of sight?

Roy darted around the back, and shouted again, "Drop the gun, or I'll shoot you."

By this time, I was standing behind Roy. As the intruder took off again, Roy shot him in the leg. Until now, the psycho had not uttered a word. But now high-pitched screams filled the air. It was obviously a woman's voice. She was raving, writhing like an animal, and reaching for her gun. Roy kicked it from her reach while she screamed over and over, "Get her. She's the bad one. Lock her up."

Meanwhile, I ran into Jean's house to see how badly she was hurt. "Jean, where are you? Are you hurt?"

Her two poodles were barking and running around, her three cats were meowing frantically, and Rod Stewart was blasting away on her stereo. I called out to her once again, "Are you hurt?"

"Hell, yes, I'm hurt," she yelled as she slipped from behind the bathroom door.

"Why didn't you stay away from the windows?"

"I was trying to, but I went around the back to see where you all went, then bang! Micki, I'm bleeding and my blouse is ruined. It hurts, it hurts—and I can't stand pain. Besides that, what kind of burglar shows up in broad daylight?"

"First things first. Let's see the damage."

Jean rolled up the sleeve of her blouse. There was a tear in her sleeve where the bullet grazed her arm. As I was cleaning and bandaging her arm, I realized I'd seen this outfit in my dream.

"You're not hurt badly. I'll drive you to the hospital so they can have a look at this. By the way, where were you headed all dressed up?"

"To the university. The psychology department chairman wanted me to come in today so we could select my classes for the fall semester."

"Be right back. Sit tight. I'll see if it's safe to go outside."

I peeked out the front door. Roy had the woman cuffed and was placing her in his patrol car. He saw me looking.

"Is Jean all right?"

"Yeah, but she's really upset. The bullet grazed her arm, and it's bleeding a lot. I wanted to make sure it was safe to come out before I took her to the hospital."

"Is she in good enough shape to identify wild thing here before I take her to the hospital?"

"I think so. I'll bring her out and see if she knows her."

We collected Jean's purse and insurance card and then walked toward Roy. The woman began screaming at the top of her lungs as Jean got closer to the car.

"You bitch, you liar. You're trying to steal my boyfriend," she wailed.

This piqued Jean's interest. When she recognized the woman, she lashed back with a fury. "Your boyfriend? You sick asshole, he was my boyfriend for eight years."

Jean and the woman exchanged a few choice words while I told Roy what I knew. The last thing I heard before we left for the hospital was Jean telling the woman, "You're sick, sick, sick, and now you're also a criminal. I'm going to press charges on you for aggravated assault, or maybe even attempted murder. I'm bleeding and you owe me a silk blouse!"

Jean was all too happy to give Roy any information he needed for his offense report. She no longer had any fiduciary duty toward the woman, and any health care or counselor's privilege was also a moot point once the woman committed a life-threatening act against Jean.

"Please have Jean come down to the station tomorrow, or as soon as she feels up to it. I'll have to write up a report, and justify why I'm making house calls."

"Sure. I hope this doesn't get you in any trouble. Thank you for coming so quickly. That woman could have killed Jean if she had gotten into her house."

"She obviously wanted to hurt her, or she wouldn't have attempted it in our presence. She's half a bubble off, Micki, maybe even more."

"Thanks again. I guess you've noticed that no one else from the precinct has arrived yet—and we called them thirty minutes ago."

"Well, you know how it is. You got the best." He grinned at me before pulling away.

It was comforting to know that I could always count on Roy. Deputy dog would always come running. He loved what he did, and that included protecting me and those I loved. I helped Jean into my car, and called the office to tell Sherry that I'd be out most of the day. I intended to stay with Jean and help her in making a report down at the police department, today if at all possible. Jean was an extraordinary procrastinator. Unless she pressed charges while she was still mad, she'd end up deciding it was too much trouble.

Once we left the house, Jean calmed down. But as we neared the hospital, she got anxious.

"What do you think they'll do?"

"The hospital or the police?"

"You know I hate hospitals."

"I'm no doctor. Have you had a tetanus shot lately?"

"God, no. I don't do needles."

"I hate to break it to you, but you may have to get some shots—tetanus, antibiotics, whatever. But don't worry, I'm here to hold your hand. And later, if you feel up to it, we'll go make that police report and have lunch. You can come with me to pick up Michael, and maybe the three of us will go to the park and feed the ducks."

"Picking up Michael and feeding the ducks sounds okay, but I don't think I need a hospital. I'm still wearing a bloody blouse. I can go to my doctor later, if I need to."

"You're not getting out of this just because you're a scaredy cat."

The hospital ordeal wasn't as bad as I'd expected. We were in and out within two hours. They did give Jean a shot. I had never seen an adult with such a phobia for needles, but it was nothing compared to her phobia for roaches. If one had crawled across the floor while they were injecting her, she would have dropped dead. She cooperated with the shot because, according to her, "it pales in comparison to the hole in my arm."

We also met Roy, much to his surprise, before noon and completed his report in time to have lunch. Jean invited him along. To my disbelief, he declined. Said he was too busy. But, before we left, he leaned over and whispered that he would call me on my digital phone later that afternoon. I kept meaning to bring up the subject of my unlisted digital number. He said he needed to see me about something. Jean and I had a quick lunch at a local deli, then we picked Michael up at school.

The three of us went to Magnolia Park. While Michael fed the ducks and entertained himself on the playground equipment, Jean and I talked about the day's events. She was still quite shaken that the nut case had actually found her house and tried to hurt her.

"Jean, remember those nightmares I was having about you?"

"I remember."

"Well, in my dreams you were wearing what you have on now."

"Micki, you've never seen this outfit. I bought it yesterday, on sale. I wanted to reward myself for leaving counseling and starting my better life as a teacher."

"I know. But I still saw it. It must have been the crazoid chasing us in Shelby—and I have to say I'm relieved your attack isn't related to this case."

Jean looked exhausted from her ordeal, so I took her home. Then Michael and I cooked burgers and fries at the house. He was watching one of his Thomas-the-Tank-Engine videos before bed. He asked me why Aunt Jean's shirt was torn and bloody today. I told him she had an accident. That seemed to satisfy him. Then Roy called and begged me to meet him and Bob tomorrow night.

"I think it's in everyone's best interest if you consult with Bob. You don't have to actually represent him, just talk to him and give him some advice. If this thing goes down bad, he can hire his own lawyer. I already told him that you were my lawyer. He wasn't real happy about that. You know what a jealous jerk he is."

"I never understood his proprietary interest in Anna and me."

"Me either."

"Okay, Roy. You've worn me down. Where and what time?"

"Neches Park. Last picnic table nearest the water. Six o'clock."

"I'll be there. Be on time. I don't want to be too late picking up Michael from my folks."

"Bob and I will both be there, dead or alive."

"You're such a funny guy."

"I can be entertaining. My tongue does tricks. He's very, very good."

"I'm happy for you, Roy."

"You don't know what you're missing. Give me a chance."

"I'll think about it."

"Think about my tongue and my lips and all the places they can kiss you and lick you."

I didn't respond. "Micki, are you there?"

"I don't know what to say."

"Don't say anything. Just think about it, long and hard. I'll see you tomorrow, six o'clock sharp."

His self-promotion annoyed me. It was a crude come-on. I had become accustomed to the tenderness of married sex with Les.

Michael and I went to sleep with the chickens. I realized how tired I was as soon as my head hit the pillow. Having one of your best friends get shot takes a lot out of you. As I fell asleep, I made two wishes: one that I didn't have bad dreams, and the other that tomorrow was less eventful.

Chapter Twenty-Four

*L*es called Thursday morning as Michael and I were getting ready. I told him about what happened at Jean's. He seemed disturbed, but I reassured him that the boogie man hadn't gotten to me or Michael.

I was at work bright and early. I anticipated a stressful, tiring day with clients coming in on the hour every hour until five o'clock. There had been too much to deal with lately, and I was not looking forward to seeing all those people with all their problems. I used to love it, but lately I yearned to get away from the practice of law, away from law enforcement, and away from other people's problems. I was beginning to see what Jean meant when she wondered what it would be like to work with people who liked their lives.

I was covered up all day, and I asked my mom to pick up Michael from school and keep him until I got in. She said she would bring him to my house if I called her when I was leaving the office. I didn't mention the meeting that I was having in the park this evening. No need to concern her. Mom knew Roy—and she had always been suspicious of his work and of his intentions toward me.

Once Sherry was gone, I called Roy and asked him to meet

me earlier so that I wouldn't risk being alone with Bob. He agreed. And he didn't mention his tongue this time, thank goodness. It sounded so stupid when he said it. Why was my interest suddenly piqued? Too much time passing between sexual encounters with my husband, I guess. While driving to the park, I reminded myself to be in control of my urges. I contemplated how maturity had helped me distinguish between genuine longing for a particular man and simple horniness.

"Hi, good-looking. Feeling better today?" Roy asked.

"No one has been shot today."

"Bob's not here yet. I hope he shows. I think he knows more than he's letting on. See if you can get anymore information out of him. He's never really liked me." I had a suspicious notion that Roy was using me to get to Bob, but I didn't know why.

"He's fucking weird, and he doesn't like anyone." I was clear about that.

"I have some interesting info for you. It seems that Susan Jeffries is hanging out with good old Glen Harding."

"Sheriff Harding?" I was amazed. Anna said Susan liked men with money.

"The one and only. I followed her one night after I left work. I found out who she was seeing the first night I tailed her. She made it easy. Every evening she goes to the same place, same time, and meets good old Glenny."

"Is he still married?"

"Sure he is. They wouldn't be hiding out at a downtown motel if he wasn't."

"That's really weird. Wayne's dead, so she can cash in on some of the hefty life insurance policies. I get that part. Jake killed him, so she probably had Jake killed to cover her tracks. I get that too. Billy Shipley's dead, and the sheriff is bedding the rich, grieving widow. That part I don't get. He's not her type."

"We need Bob to tie all this up for us. It does appear that the sheriff's office, or at least the sheriff, is involved in this. It makes sense that his department would keep information from the police about the burglaries that Jake did to protect Susan. Harding wouldn't want Jake to give information on Susan's involvement in Wayne's murder.

"I'm sure they're all afraid to spend money and attract the FBI's attention. After all, the case was never closed, and they really want that money. The statute of limitations on Jake's house burglaries has run. Something must have happened between Susan, Sheriff Glenny, and Jake. The money must have become a problem for them to have killed Jake. It had to have been Susan and Glen."

Bob came roaring up in a rental car, blasted out of the front seat, and almost tripped and fell before reaching us at the picnic table.

"You're wound pretty tight this evening." Roy laughed at Bob's approach.

"You would be too if you were in my shoes, copper boy."

Bob never liked Roy, maybe because he was younger, better looking, more successful with the ladies.

Bob looked over at me and said, "I appreciate you coming, Micki."

"You can thank Roy that I'm here. He convinced me to come and listen to you. Before we begin, we have one matter to clarify. Under no circumstances will I acquiesce and be your attorney. But I will be your consulting attorney, and I may give you legal advice."

"So that means that you couldn't testify against me?" He raised his eyebrows.

"That's right. Anything you tell me would be privileged." I don't know why I felt compelled to help him.

"Okay, here goes. Jake was hired to kill Wayne. Jake blackmailed me, so I hid evidence in the Jeffries case that would have nailed Jake's coffin shut. As gravy, he offered me half a million dollars. By the way, I haven't seen one red cent of that money. Susan wanted to wait until the case was officially closed. I've waited years. It didn't matter much to me when I got my money, as long as it was before I retired.

"The District Attorney didn't have enough evidence to convict Jake. Recently they sent Susan a letter telling her as much. Well, this put her mind at rest. She wanted Jake to pay me out of his million and a half. But he said he didn't risk his hairy ass for her for a piddling million, when she had seven and a half million.

So he upped the ante. Said since it had been him taking all the risks and her that had come out rich and lily white, he now wanted three million. Double or nothing, or he'd talk"

Bob paused. Roy had some burning questions.

"So Bob, when did Jake tell you about this meeting with Susan?"

"A few weeks ago. Jake was madder than a hatter when he came by the beach cabin."

"Was it apparent to you where your share was coming from?"

"Not really, but he assured me that I would get paid no matter what. It was because of me he didn't have to spend the rest of his life in jail or face the death penalty."

"So, you were getting half a million for evidence tampering?"

"Basically, yes."

"Did Susan agree to pay Jake the three million?"

"He said she did, but then he came up dead, all carved up. I don't care about the money anymore. I want to retire and live without the fear of ending up like Jake. Life in prison would be a relief compared to what happened to him."

"Tell us about the sheriff," I demanded.

"What do you mean?"

"I mean tell us about him and Susan." I made an obscene gesture referring to the sex act.

"How did you know about that?"

"I followed Susan." Roy interjected.

"Shit, Roy, you're going to cause us all to be shredded into boudain." Bob was fond of cajun sausage. I couldn't imagine why he wouldn't want to enter the food chain as sausage and rice.

"Why is that, Bob?" I could sense that Roy was pissed that Bob was insinuating he put us all in danger.

"Because the sheriff is calling the shots now, that's why. He killed Billy Shipley when he got too close to the truth. The poor bastard, he never knew what hit him, bullet to the brain."

"What else?" Roy asked.

"I'm fairly positive that the sheriff killed Jake, too. I'm the remaining survivor in all of this, and I'm ready to turn myself in to save my skin. That's why I wanted Micki here. I want to know what steps to take and in what order to take them."

"You want to turn yourself into the FBI?" I was incredulous.

"Well, I don't know who to turn myself into."

"How long has the sheriff been involved with Susan?" I asked.

"Since before Wayne was murdered. I'm fairly certain that Glen helped Susan with her scheme to get rid of Wayne and grab hold of his money."

"Where or how on earth did Susan meet Glen?" I had a lot of questions now.

"Jake told me they met at a rodeo. Huntsville. Remember the prison rodeos they used to have?"

"I went to a few, but they don't have them anymore."

"No, but when they did the sheriff always made a big deal over them. He would go down there and act like the big dog law enforcement type he was. Jake told me years ago that he over-heard Glen and Susan talking one night about their first rodeo. It was where they met. It was love at first buck. They bragged about screwing while sitting on top of a rhinestone-saddled horse in the back of one of the horse trailers. Pretty weird for my taste."

"So they've been an item since?" Roy asked.

"Pretty much. They've had their differences, but I think Susan wants her stud, and Glen wants her money. Glen plans to divorce his wife once the heat is off."

"No one knows about them?" I couldn't believe it.

"Oh, I think there are those that do."

"And now you believe the sheriff is after you?" Roy asked.

"I'm all that's standing in his way. He knows that I know about all three murders. I can tie him and Susan up sideways with the blackmail scheme and the murders. Do you have any idea what prison would do to a sheriff who's done what he has?"

"Probably the same thing they're going do to you." Roy guf-fawed.

"Not if I can help it, and you're in this too, Roy."

"No, I'm out of it, Bob. Jake is never going to be retried. Dead people don't go to trial, and there's nothing you can make me do now. I'm going forward with this investigation. When it's complete, then I'll make a full statement regarding your black-mail scheme against me. Fortunately, I've done nothing—nothing but talk to you. I never had to 'forget about certain evidence' in Wayne's case to protect the lives of my children. I never told you I would withhold evidence at Jake's retrial. We all assumed that he would be retried within the year of his mistrial—that is, until the judge died."

"If I tell Glenny you're involved, then you'll do whatever I say if you know what's good for you."

"If you do that, then I'll take you in right now and assure myself that you never see that bastard again."

"All right, all right. I don't need you anyway. Jake's dead, and I don't have to protect him or my investment anymore. It looks like I'll never see my money."

"It's not your money," Roy snorted. "Why would Jake pay you anything if he could blackmail you?"

"You know what I mean. I had plans for the money. Jake wasn't sure he could prove anything against me. He just made idle threats about certain drugs and prostitutes. He knew that the money would keep me quiet. All he had on me was hearsay, nothing he could prove to the DA."

"Get over it. And another thing, old man, if you ever threaten me again or harm my children, you will never see the light of another day. Do I make myself crystal-clear? I'm not afraid of you anymore, I've pieced enough of this together to realize you're too much of a coward to be scared of. Hell, your drinking alone makes you incompetent."

I interrupted their power struggle. "We've established that you no longer need Roy, and Roy has technically done nothing wrong. Where do we go from here?" I looked at both of them.

"That's what I had hoped you could tell me," Bob admitted.

"I can't tell you what to do. You have to tell me how you want this to end. Give me some details about the blackmail and why it is that you were vulnerable to all of this."

"That's a sordid little story."

"Of course. Why wouldn't it be?"

"There's no need for sarcasm. I'm in real danger, and I know the sheriff will use what he knows about me to cut a deal, if he has to."

"What does he know about you?" I asked again.

"I was running prostitutes at Belle, providing recreational drugs and porn, that kind of thing. I flew in rich guys from all over the country, had them fed and fucked. It was a profitable scheme for a while. The sheriff looked the other way because of my connection to the Jeffries case. He's going to use it now. He's going to be desperate if I tell everything I know."

"How can that stuff hurt you? It only means that you will do anything for money. Besides Belle is on the Texas/Louisiana border. And what's a little prostitution and drugs among friends? Anything goes there! *Laissez les bon temps roulet*!"

"He'll try to frame me for Jake's murder. He'll say that I killed him because Jake never paid me."

"What makes you think he'll do that?"

"Jake warned me just before he was killed that Glen was looking to pin all of this on me and him, and then take us out. Make himself out to be some kind of hero by solving a controversial old case. That would leave him and Susan to enjoy Wayne's insurance proceeds without the added complication of a paper trail between them and Jake and me. They wouldn't have to worry down the line that Jake or I would talk."

I was beginning to get nauseated listening to his sleazy story. It was getting late, so I asked Bob again, "What do you want the end result to be?"

"I want to be alive when all of this comes to a head."

"Is that all you want?"

"I prefer not to spend any time in prison either."

Roy looked disgusted and told Bob as much. "You don't want much, do you, asshole?"

I interrupted. "Now that's asking a lot, because the way I see it, the District Attorney will want to make an example of you."

"That's why I'm here talking to you. I want to know how to stay alive and keep out of prison. What should I do?"

"Roy will need to turn you in, recommend that they go easy on you because you'll be the state's star witness. You'll need to hire the best criminal defense expert in town to escort you to jail, get your bond set, and cut your deal. Avoid talking to the feds, and give the newspaper a headline to protect you from anyone out there looking to do you in. Finally, place yourself in protective custody until the trial. They might try Susan and Glen separately because of the political and social implications. I have a suspicion that there may be others involved with this much money floating around. People can't seem to keep their mouths shut when the money is flowing."

"I don't know if I'm ready to turn state's evidence yet." Bob glared at Roy. He didn't trust Roy after threatening him and his kids. Hell, he despised cops, especially pretty-boy Roy.

"What are you waiting for? The money?" I asked.

"Not anymore. I don't want to be first in line with the feds."

"Where are they keeping all the millions, Bob?"

"Susan invested some of it, hid some out of the country, hid some at Belle. It's all over the place. She made sure no one but her could get their hands on it."

It was all beginning to come together now: the cash, the books, and the ledgers Anna found at Belle. They were Bob's. He kept his dirty money in the wall safe in the master bedroom.

"Say, Bob, where did all the bones and blood in the barn at Belle come from?" I had to ask.

"The girls played some interesting games with the men I had flown in. We advertised an erotic voodoo ceremony in the bayou in big papers like the *New York Times*. These same high rollers would come back month after month. It gave me enough money to hang onto my Belle. The old farts we flew in particularly loved the mambos, the female priests. They would feast before the main ceremony, create a pattern of cornmeal on the floor, then shake rattles, beat drums, and chant. The mambos would call Ezili, the female spirit of love, and then the guys would enjoy a nice orgy. To complete the voodoo ceremony, the ladies would summon Baka, a live spirit who took the form of an animal. They would sacrifice a goat, sheep, or chicken—and then dance like they were possessed. The grand finale was when all present drank from a chalice of blood."

"I'll ask you again. Where did all the blood and bones come from?"

"I saved them over the years, the bones that is. I sort of collected them from old cases, and they came in handy for the voodoo games. The blood—well, I'd take a little from the lab for the girls to paint with, all part of the bayou allure."

I winced. "Sorry I asked. So most of Anna's blood testing was in vain?"

"I'm afraid so." Bob hung his head. He looked uncharacteristically ashamed.

"I never meant for her to work so hard for nothing, but I couldn't tell her about all this. She'd hate me." If she didn't hate him by now, she never would.

Roy seemed to wake up, and he jumped to his feet. "Hey Bob, who fired shots at me that first day at Belle?"

"Glenny had Jake go over and try to scare everyone away so he could remove the money that Susan had hidden at Belle. He also wanted me to sanitize the place, clean up after the girls, and get rid of trace evidence. By the time Jake got out to Belle, it was too late. You all were finished for the day. It was an error in judgment for him to shoot at you, Roy."

Roy spit on the ground. "Thanks. That makes me feel a lot better."

I remembered Anna found a lot of cash at Belle. I'd have to check with her to see if she got around to counting it.

"Think about what we talked about, Bob, and go hire yourself a good lawyer. Get more legal advice and turn yourself in. Don't wait too long. Someone else may get in line ahead of you and give the state and the feds the information they're looking for. Or you may be full of embalming fluid and unable to testify if you wait too long."

Bob sighed, then spoke. "I'll think about it this weekend and call Roy if I get the courage to turn myself in by Monday."

"You better find the courage, Bob. I have a responsibility to bring this evidence forward, and I will. You have until Monday to find a lawyer, and I expect you and the mouthpiece you hire to be at the courthouse no later than ten o'clock Monday morning," Roy threatened.

"I hear you."

"If you skip out on me, I'll spill your little story for you, and then you'll have no hope of getting probation. Your ass will be in the penitentiary where it belongs. I'm only cutting you a little slack for old times' sake, because we used to work on the same side of the law." Roy was holding his gag reflex.

"I'll be there, and thanks for the break. I owe you one."

"You don't owe me anything. Once this is over, I want nothing more to do with you."

"Ditto," I echoed.

"You don't think very highly of me, do you?"

"No, never did," Roy said.

Bob appeared genuinely hurt and astonishingly sober. Once he left, I felt more comfortable. Roy and I sat on the picnic table and watched the tugboats maneuver down the river. It was beginning to get dark. Dusk was my favorite time of day. It meant that the day was finished, the pressure was off, and worries were few, until daylight came again. We sat in silence for awhile. Roy stepped over to his car and withdrew a small ice chest. It contained a few Cokes, two plastic cups, some Bacardi rum, and a lime. He mixed a Cuba Libre. Without asking, he gave me one too.

"Thank you, I need this."

"Me, too." He sighed.

We sat and talked about old times, drank one, two, three, four Cuba Libres. Then, without warning, Roy leaned over and kissed me. I guess the booze gave him courage.

"Wow," was all I could say.

"It's easier for me to ask your forgiveness than your permission." He laughed easily.

"There's nothing to forgive. I've been thinking about us doing that for days."

"What else have you thought about us doing?"

"Let your imagination run wild." I smiled and looked him up and down.

By then the alcohol had taken full effect. I'd lost both my sense of decorum and my better judgment. Roy had an unbelievable hard-on. He lay me down on the picnic table, leaned over me, and began kissing my neck. Unbuttoning my dress, he realized I wasn't wearing a bra and went a little crazy. He began kissing and licking my breasts. My head was spinning from all the liquor I'd consumed in such a short time, but I could still feel the pressure of the picnic table against my head and back. Roy covered me with his body and began kissing me with urgency. My head stopped spinning, and I found myself kissing him back with equal passion. He picked me up and said, "No, we're going to do this right. We've waited so long." He carried me in his arms a few more feet and then put me down next to a huge pecan tree near his car.

"What's wrong, Roy? Am I too heavy?"

"You're perfect." He began kissing me again. Then he whispered in my ear, "I'm not going to make it to my house. I'm losing my mind."

He unbuttoned my dress all the way. Roy kissed my abdomen, knelt down in front of me, and began licking me.

"I'm not going to make it to your house either, Roy."

With his head buried between my legs, my head up against the tree, and my hands pulling him closer to me, my breathing turned to panting. Roy stood up momentarily, unbuttoned his jeans, and I pulled IT out. He picked me up, held my bottom with his two hands, then leaned me against the tree, and entered me. We were thrusting against one another with the tree hiding us from anyone entering the park. It was dark now, and we were oblivious to anyone else in the park—or anyone in the universe, for that matter. I felt a little silly and I told Roy, "I hope the local cops aren't out looking for teenagers tonight."

He laughed and said, "Who cares?"

"You will if it keeps you from making chief."

"Don't worry. We'll go somewhere a little more discreet if you like."

"I like."

"Promise me you won't change your mind before we get to my place."

"There's no turning back now."

Roy buttoned my dress and his jeans, and we left in his car. We drove to his house just a few minutes away. He carried me in. I wasn't sure about all the caveman antics, but it felt good to be carried. He turned down the bed in his room, left momentarily, and reentered with two drinks.

"I don't want you to get an attack of conscience."

"If it's something that I want to do, who's going to stop me?"

"No one here is stopping you." He squeezed lime the entire length of my right leg and licked it off. When he reached my crotch, he began to lick me very gently, then more vigorously. I reached down and unbuttoned his pants, then placed my mouth over his hardness and positioned myself over his face. When he could take it no longer, he rolled over and entered me.

"God, you feel good," I told him.

"And you are so fine, just like I knew you would be," he murmured. We were consumed for hours. During our gymnastics I caught a glimpse of the time on Roy's clock radio. It was ten o'clock.

"Roy, look at the time. I've got to get out of here. I have to pick up Michael. What the hell am I going to tell my parents?"

"Take it easy. I'll drive you back to your car."

I dressed quickly. Roy pushed me back on the bed, fell on top of me, and began kissing me again. I went with it for a few minutes, and then remembered who I was and where I was supposed to be.

"Let's go. What the hell kind of story am I going to have to make up about this?"

"You'll think of something lawyerly."

"I will?"

"Sure. You were working and time slipped away."

Roy drove me back to the park and walked me to my car. He opened my door. Once I was behind the wheel, he looked down at me and whispered something I couldn't hear.

"What?" I asked.

"Nothing. You don't want to hear it."

"Yes, I do."

"I love you, I always have. I just couldn't admit it before."

"I know, Roy—and I don't know what to say or what to do."

He was right. I didn't want to hear it, it was too late. Seducing him had been wrong. I had no intention of devastating my life because of a thirteen-year-old physical attraction. As a matter of fact, it was now me who needed the bayou privilege because Roy now had the power to destroy my marriage.

"It's okay. Whatever you decide is okay with me. Be careful. I'll call you tomorrow."

"Les will be in for my family reunion this weekend." I gave him a wistful look and left with tears in my eyes. As I drove away, I hoped he understood my predicament. I hoped he would respect my feelings for my family. I hadn't anticipated the sex inviting old feelings between Roy and me. I thought I could just have sex with him and feel good knowing it was just sex. I had a suspicion it was going to take me a while to sort everything out. Why did life have to be so damn complicated? All of a sudden I realized how much Les meant to me, Les who would never cheat on me for anything.

My digital phone rang. It was Mom. She wanted to know if I was ready for her to bring Michael home. When I pulled in my driveway, she was waiting. Michael looked so tired, I felt horrible about leaving him so late. He was such a little fellow, and he tired out after a day of school. I should have been home earlier. Gathering him in my arms, I kissed Mom goodbye. Although my mother was very critical of me at times, she was still my champion. Next to Les and Michael, I loved her most in the world. I was relieved that she hadn't asked me where I had been or why I was so late. Lying was not a talent of mine. Michael was so sleepy that we skipped our bedtime story. After tucking him in, I dialed Anna's number.

"Still up?" I asked her.

"Of course I'm up. I don't go to bed this early."

"I know you get up early, so I assumed you went to bed with the chickens too."

"Not before the ten o'clock news. Hell, we may be on it. Never know these days."

"That's why I called. It looks like Bob will make the Monday evening news, and the paper. Roy and I met with him tonight."

"I thought you weren't going to meet with him anymore?"

"Roy changed my mind for me. Bob is the only one who has firsthand knowledge about this mystery. Have you got any amazing lab results yet?"

"They're amazing, all right. I have so many different blood types, semen stains, and hairs that it looks like an entire community stayed at Belle."

"That's possible."

"What do you mean?"

"Tonight Bob admitted that he was running whores, drugs, and porn at Belle. In addition to that, he used old blood and old bones from previous lab cases in some kind of voodoo ritual. That compromises your results."

"No shit?"

"No shit. Don't you just hate him?" I knew she didn't. It was a rhetorical question.

"Yes, I do. Gosh, Micki, it will be so tough to get any meaningful results with commingled trace evidence. I won't know what might be related to the murders and what might be related to Bob's extracurricular activities. The blood stains could be a by-product of S&M, murder, or drunken accidents. This means the semen stains are not likely to be related to the murders. None of it correlates with Wayne, Billy, or Jake. I've been wasting my time, not to mention the expense of the DNA testing. Bob may have promoted me and trained me, but it sure does piss me off that he jerked me around."

"Don't look at it that way. You know that every moment you spend eliminating suspects or irrelevant trace evidence is time well spent. What about the ballistics testing?"

"Now, that is more conclusive. I almost burned up the firing box testing the nine millimeter weapons in this case. And I nearly drowned myself firing into that tall tube of water."

"Tell me what you found out."

"The gun from the beach is the one that killed Wayne, as we thought all along. I matched the lands and grooves of the known shells microscopically with the three unknown shells removed from the body. When I fired the known shells into the firing box, I caught the cotton on fire. It was a pretty hot load, and guess what else? I raised the serial number with nitric acid. It matches the serial number of a nine millimeter registered to Susan Jeffries, purchased just days before Wayne's murder." I told Anna the story just as Roy had told it to me. She was dumb-founded about Susan's and the sheriff's relationship.

"Good old sheriff must have covered that up prior to trial. Susan wasn't even a suspect," Anna marveled.

"What about the gun you found in the well at the mansion?"

I asked.

"The bullet found in Billy's skull matched bullets fired from that gun. So at least we know where those two guns fit in."

"I still don't understand why Bob didn't throw that gun as far into the water as he could, or bury it. It would have rusted, and the sand and surf would have covered it up within a few hours. It probably never would have been found." Anna sounded sad. I knew what she was thinking. If Bob had gotten rid of the gun he wouldn't be in so much trouble. She still protected him. He must have some endearing quality that escaped me.

"True, but our hero was either saving it for his own personal use, or didn't have the guts to actually destroy the evidence. He wouldn't have left himself a map unless he intended to dig it up at some later date. He's such a liar. We'll never know what his real intentions were. At this moment he's trying to save his own skin. He's afraid he's next in line at the morgue." I listened for her reaction.

"Is that so? Serves him right. Does he have the missing evidence?" She didn't mean it. I could hear it in her voice.

"You know, I didn't think to ask him. Not a very good cross-examination, I guess. You can ask him yourself after he turns himself into the police on Monday."

"He what?"

"He's turning state's evidence. He's afraid if he doesn't that he'll end up in prison—that is, if Glen and Susan don't kill him first."

"You're not representing him, are you?"

"Not hardly, and it looks like Roy won't be needing my help either."

"Why not?"

"Bob never got him to do anything illegal, not that he didn't try. Anna, he was threatening to hurt Roy's kids. Can you believe that?"

"At this point, I can believe anything. But I don't think macho Roy is easily intimidated."

"Did you hear about Jean?" I ignored her comment regarding Roy.

"I heard. And here's something that will interest you. It seems that the sedan that followed you and Jean to Shelby, the one you thought might be the feds—well, it was that crazy lady following Jean. Isn't that a hoot?"

I sighed with relief. I suspected as much. Maybe I had been a little paranoid, accepting responsibility for all the strange goings-on lately.

"I shot at her car, Anna. Why would she risk coming for Jean again so soon after that?"

"She's crazy as a bedbug. Not to change the subject, but how much detail did Bob give you about Wayne's murder? I know he's knee-deep in it."

"Plenty." Then I related the whole sordid scheme to Anna. It took me awhile to finish the tale, and all Anna could say when I was finished was, "He sold his soul for five hundred thousand dollars?"

"He did, and Anna, you cannot divulge any of this, ever. I agreed to be Bob's consulting attorney. I can't talk about it either. I'd love to testify against him, but my ethical duty prevents it. I'm telling you because you work for him, and you need to protect yourself."

Anna's voice screeched. "He said all of that in front of a police officer?"

We both knew what that meant. Roy could testify against him. Bob volunteered the information to a cop, and he wasn't under arrest at the time. So *Miranda* didn't apply.

"What about information I overheard when Bob and Roy met at the lab, is that confidential?"

"No, it's not. What did you hear?"

"Some of what you heard today. What if they call me to testify?"

"If you're subpoenaed, then you'll have to testify." The law was clear on some things at least.

"As much as I hate what he's done, I don't want to hurt him."

"I know. It would complicate your life and encourage an early retirement."

"It makes me sad that three greedy people killed my friend."

"I know this is hard for you, since you knew him so well. Listen, let's not talk about it anymore, and you go on to bed now. Sleep if you can. I'll talk to you on Monday. I have a reunion this weekend down at the park, and I'll be busy with Les and family."

"Tell Les I said hello."

"I will, and let me know if any of the evidence reveals some unexpected surprises."

"Goodnight, Micki."

Chapter Twenty-Five

I showered and turned on some music. My compact disc player shuffled discs back and forth, playing selections from the
Moody Blues, the Guess Who, the Rolling Stones, Creedence
Clearwater Revival, Journey, and Led Zeppelin. There was something heady about music from the seventies that I liked. After all,
I grew up with it. I dreamed all night about Roy and me having
sex. It was more intense each time I dreamed it, damn it to hell.

I arrived at the courthouse early Friday morning and filed my
own motions and pleadings. Sherry had taken a day of vacation.

Back at the office the first thing I did was check the messages,
next I returned the phones to the answering service. No way was
I battling the calls all day. I completed some research on search
and seizure, answered some discovery in a divorce case, and went
to have lunch with Michael.

It was parents day, and you brought a box lunch for you and
your child. We sat under the marvelous magnolia trees on a blanket and watched the older children put on a play. Michael was
mesmerized by their rendition of *Cats*. Maybe he'd be a veterinarian some day. That would be a pleasant occupation. Whatever
he did, I wanted him to be happy.

We had a fun lunch, and he kissed me on the cheek before I

took him back to the office with me. He looked at books I kept in my office for him and colored on some of my legal pads. I made some phone calls and organized my files for Monday morning. About five o'clock we left and stopped by the grocery store. He loved shopping.

"Mommy, can we buy me a new car?" He was crazy about miniature cars, the tinier the better.

"How about two new cars?"

"Wow, two?"

"Sure, you haven't bought any new ones since you went to Colorado, have you?"

"They didn't have them at the stores where Daddy went."

"That's too bad. We don't want you to be deprived, do we?"

"No," he said, as if he understood perfectly.

I picked up some steaks and wine for dinner: a couple of ribeyes and two bottles of Piesporter. Les and I had never adhered to the "reds with meat and whites with fish" routine. We drank what we liked, and we didn't like the reds.

The bag boy who followed me home a while back gave me a funny look when he saw Michael. So much for his infatuation, short-lived like everything else in life. But that's not true any-more, I thought to myself. My love for Michael, Les, my family, and my friends was forever. I realized how much happier I was than I used to be.

It occurred to me that my lusty interest in Roy was related to the need to finish old business. No matter how great it was, it was now part of my past. This moment of insight into my emotional growth and maturity made me absolutely certain that there was no future for me with Roy. I was where I needed to be and with whom I wanted to spend the rest of my life. Michael was looking up at me as I came out of my fog.

"Come on, sweetie. Help me with the groceries. We need to get them home and pick up Daddy at the airport."

"It's today?" He squealed with joy.

"It's today. Are you excited about seeing him?"

"I want him to come home," he replied.

"So do I, so do I," I repeated.

We dropped the groceries by the house and drove to the airport. There was Les standing on the curb just outside the baggage pickup. He looked wonderful, tall and handsome, and happy to see us.

"I thought you didn't get in for another hour. Michael and I were going to walk around the airport and wait for you."

"I caught an earlier flight out. I knew you'd be here early." He grinned from ear to ear.

"Oh, you did? How did you know that?"

"I know you." I knew I could trust him to have a mischievous response.

He kissed me, and leaned over to pick up Michael. He swung him around and around.

"How's my big boy? Have you been taking care of your Mom for me?"

"Yes, I have. I got two new cars today. See." He extended a hand filled with a green truck and a blue four-wheeler. He was into trucks these days.

"Very nice."

"I bought some steaks and wine for dinner, are you hungry?"

"Starved, nothing worse than airline food, except maybe hospital food."

On the drive home, the three of us all crowded into the front seat. Once there, we unpacked Les' clothes, fixed dinner, and relaxed in the back yard. After putting Michael to bed, we concocted our dishes for the upcoming reunion. We made broccoli cheese rice—we called it green rice—and a huge fruit salad. I fed Les peaches, his favorite fruit, and he fed me mine, strawberries.

Cooking together was sensual, and we touched frequently and longingly. It was refreshing to have a conversation and be able to watch the expression on each other's faces. I missed that when he was away and we only spoke over the telephone. Les and I slept spooned together. My fling with Roy left me racked with guilt, but I couldn't think about it then. I blamed the wine for causing Les and me to fall asleep so early. However, in the wee hours of the morning he woke me. In his aroused state he slowly took me from behind. I was still in a wine-state, slightly asleep and very relaxed. I knew I could never give him up, never. I made my decision when I met him, even before I said, "till death do us part." I smiled lazily and went back to sleep with his arm around my waist. Michael got up very early the next morning and jumped in the middle of our bed. We all showered, dressed, and picked up my parents. My three brothers were attending the reunion, but you never knew when, with whom, or how they would show up.

"Will we all fit?" my mom asked.

"Sure we will. Get in," my father commanded.

I opened the back of the sport utility vehicle. Les and I bought it last year. It would hold a small tribe.

The drive was short, about ten minutes. When we got there, we couldn't believe the crowd. At least five hundred people were in attendance. Some came early because they lived out of town, they set up their tables earlier this morning. We got there right about lunch time, as my Dad insisted. He was always on time and you had better be as well. More importantly, he always ate his meals at the same time each day.

I saw my grandfather dancing with a young woman. He had always had an eye for the ladies. A French band was playing Cajun music. Rock and roll was more my taste, but the older generation loved it. You could hear an "Aaaaiii-yeee" every now and then. Grandpa waltzed over and grabbed my hand. When I was just a little girl, he had taught me how to waltz, jitterbug, and polka. They were fun dances and required a lot of energy. I don't know where he found the stamina at his age. As we waltzed, I thought about how I'd always loved dancing with him. He had a folksy charisma that everyone admired. My father looked a lot like him, but they had very different temperaments. Michael stood back and watched us in amazement. He didn't like dancing yet. Les was already eating, his favorite pastime.

Mom was unwrapping our dishes and placing serving utensils in all of them. Dad was busy greeting his several hundred relatives. I asked myself how a family could be this big. And this wasn't all of them. I'm certain that this oppressive crowd of relatives horrified my mother, who was an only child and had a relatively small family tree. But she loved my Dad's family, and they loved her. She was an original: tall, beautiful, intelligent, talented, and outspoken. Well, maybe they didn't always like the outspoken part of her personality, but they respected it.

As I was doing a fadodo with granddad, others joined in. The music was getting livelier, and the mood was rising as well, probably something to do with the amount of liquor being consumed. Then I made my way back to Les and loaded plates of food for the three of us.

"I can't believe all the food," Les exclaimed.

"Most of Dad's relatives do like to cook." There was enough food here to feed a small army. We ate and gabbed with some of the cousins close to my age and then moved on to some people I had never met before. Some of the relatives were pretty remote, but I got a sense of connectedness. It helped me understand my Dad better, seeing him in the context of his family.

My brothers finally showed up, separately of course. They wouldn't be caught dead together. I saw my eldest brother flirting with some of our teenage cousins. My youngest brother was guzzling down all the beer he could find. And my middle brother, the most intelligent and outrageous of the bunch, was telling the "bullwhip" story on my parents. One Christmas, Santa Claus gave each of my three brothers nice leather bullwhips. After the holidays it was unfortunate for us, the four heathen children, that the whips were usually handy for corporal punishment. One time my mother chased Dale around in the garage with a bullwhip in her right hand and a chair in her left hand. She looked like an animal trainer, and I'm certain she felt like one. What mother with four young children wouldn't? Mom and Dad laughed as if he was joking. It gave me a bittersweet feeling, and I knew my parents needed to make light of it.

Les and I stuffed ourselves. Michael, on the other hand, wanted to go swimming at the pool located in the park. We excused ourselves for about an hour and took him swimming. Once we got back to the reunion, we realized that we were the only sober couple there. So we decided to leave and spend what remained of the day quietly at home. Mom and Dad decided to remain awhile with my grandparents. The three of us went home and rented a video. The remainder of the weekend went by swiftly. Before I knew it, I was driving Les to the airport.

"Please hurry home," I begged him.

"I will. It's all downhill now. We can spend the summer traveling if you can take some time off. How about France, or maybe Italy?" he asked. Les loved to travel, maybe too much.

"Sounds great to me." What could I say? Who wouldn't love to see Europe?

Michael was clinging to Les now. He looked as if he was going to cry.

"Take care of Mamma for me, Michael."

"I will," he fretted.

Les kissed us both good-bye and walked away. I felt abandoned, even though I knew it was foolish. I was old enough not to feel this way, but I still felt the emptiness when he left. It never seemed to bother Les to leave. He seemed to like being away at work and around others. We were different that way. Les made decisions easily, where I agonized over them. Driving Michael home I thought about the weekend reunion and how being with several generations of family put things in perspective. It helped to see how I got to be who I was, good and bad.

Chapter Twenty-Six

"Let's get you to school, Michael." He didn't answer.

"Want to go to the baseball game tonight?" I asked him.

"Could we?" He jumped up and down.

I wanted something to cheer us up since Les left. Michael waved good-bye from the steps of the school. I watched him until he disappeared into the building and out of sight.

I drove to my office and parked. Sherry was waiting for me, all refreshed from her three-day weekend.

"How was the beach?" I asked.

"A little windy, but warm and sunny. The cabin was cute, and I collected some great sea shells."

"Sounds nice. What's on the agenda today?"

"The usual—saving poor wretches who don't deserve our efforts."

"Which thankless victims will grace us with their presence today?"

"Mr. Remmick will be here this morning to explain why he grabbed an undercover cop's crotch in the park last week. Guess his hormones got the better of him again."

"I love those sting operations. They always bring in a lot of business."

"Monkey business," she giggled.

"I should get a new slogan for my business cards: "Dragon Slayer and Defender of Perverts.""

Sherry grinned. "We've had a real run on deviant sex cases lately, haven't we?"

"I'm beginning to think it's become our specialty. I don't know how to feel about it."

"It pays my salary. I don't mind." I paid her well, and she was worth it.

"They're entertaining, and they keep us amused, in contrast to the divorces and depressing family law cases we take."

"No shit. If we never took another one of those it would be too soon." Sherry sighed.

"My sentiments exactly. What would you think if we only took criminal cases? At least for awhile."

"That would be fine. We have plenty of criminal work. If we stop spending all of our time answering discovery and taking depositions in divorce cases, it would free us up to take more criminal cases."

"It's settled then. We'll finish the family law cases we have, and once they're disposed of we won't take anymore. It'll probably take about six months if we don't end up in trial on any of them. Let's request mediation in any case that looks remotely headed for trial. Maybe we can head off any litigation that would tie us to these civil cases for years to come."

"I'll file motions requesting mediation in the oldest ones, or the most troublesome ones, right away."

Sherry and I reviewed civil cases all day. I didn't tell her about my anticipated hiatus this summer. I would keep her working and give her a long vacation when I returned. Once we figured out where we stood with our civil cases, I cruised over to the courthouse to get plea bargains from the DA in a few criminal cases.

It had completely slipped my mind that Bob was expected to turn himself in today. Everyone was talking about it, and when I slipped into the Assistant District Attorney Alan's office, unnoticed by the secretaries, he walked in, grabbed me by the arm, and led me into a private conference room.

"Did you know about this?"

"I just found out about the malfeasance—and yes, I told him to turn himself in."

"Did you also know that our office won't be prosecuting him? It's the feds' case?"

"Yep. I know that too."

"Why wouldn't our office have jurisdiction?"

"Because there are others involved that you haven't heard about yet. Besides, if the feds decide to investigate something, that's all it takes. Makes no sense to me, but it's always been that way."

"Who else is involved?"

"Can't tell you that at present. I don't represent Bob, but I was his consulting attorney. I gave him a bayou promise that he would have a bayou privilege where I'm concerned."

"A what? What the hell is a bayou privilege?"

"It will become clear to you once the trial, or trials, begin."

"Trials? Will there be more than one?"

"If my guess is accurate, there will be at least two trials. Bob won't be tried. They'll plead him out for some lesser included offense with no jail time. It's the feds' only hope of getting the real culprits in the Jeffries case."

"Come on, tell me what's going on. The whole courthouse has been in an uproar since he gave his statement and turned himself in. It was like there was an intercom in the jail speaking directly into our office, that's how quick we heard about it."

"That's unusual. I thought it would be real hush-hush."

"Well, it's not, and Mr. District Attorney himself is livid that the feds have control over this case. They made no bones about it. They showed up this morning and took all the files and evidence from the prior trial. That is, except one folder of evidence I saw on Mack's desk a few minutes ago. He asked me to lock it in the vault and ask no questions."

"What's in it?"

"You have to answer at least one of my questions if I answer yours."

"Fair enough, what do you want to know? Anything that is not privileged I'll tell you."

"Name, names."

"Can't do that, but I will give you a hint. Someone close to Wayne Jeffries, and her illustrious boyfriend are the killers. He holds a political office as we speak. Your turn." Alan frowned.

"I locked up an envelope with evidence from the lab. A pair of shoes, some fingerprint evidence, that kind of stuff."

"Very interesting that your boss would conceal evidence from the FBI. What do you think that means?"

"I have no idea, and I will take no part in it." Alan was dazed and confused.

"What did you do with the stuff?"

"I put it in the vault like he told me to, and that's my story."

"Let me shed a little light on this issue, since you're my friend. That particular evidence never made it to the first trial. I know that for a fact because I was working at the lab when it was collected. It disappeared sometime prior to trial. Bob saw to that. It appears that your boss is perpetuating the tradition of concealing evidence in the Jeffries case."

"Why the hell would he do that?"

"Why does Mr. DA, Mack Nobles, do anything? To feather his nest and assist his climb to the legislature. Money, it all comes down to money. It takes a lot of money to fund a successful campaign."

"Are you going to use this information, Micki?"

"When I have to. Look, Alan, we've been looking for that evidence for days."

"We?"

"I've been helping Anna. She was short-handed, and I stepped in. I had to. I'll probably be forced to testify too. After all, I was the forensic chemist who made the crime scene in the original murder case. I know the feds will subpoena me."

"Great, where does that leave me? I know about the shoes and everything."

"Maybe you should talk to a lawyer."

"I thought that I was."

"Maybe we can work through this facet of it together. I thought that I was otherwise engaged as an attorney for an individual in law enforcement who had a collateral problem, but it resolved itself. I don't see any reason that I can't consult with you.

Besides, it will save you money. You know how tight you are. You wouldn't pay another lawyer anyway." I found myself thinking about the lunches and dinners I had bought this guy. He never once returned the favor, considered himself a poor government servant.

"You're right. I wouldn't pay anyone."

Then I took care of the plea bargains that brought me to the courthouse in the first place. When I left Alan, I was in a mildly agitated state. It was more than puzzling that Mack was hiding evidence from the feds. Now that Bob had come forward, the DA was playing games. It didn't add up. Something else was going on, something Bob wasn't privy to.

Walking back to my office, it occurred to me that I should call Anna and tell her she had been without a boss, since about noon, when he turned himself in.

"Are you sitting down?" I asked.

"I am now."

"Your boss turned himself in a couple of hours ago."

"That creep. He could have at least come in and cleared up a few matters of business before he abandoned me."

"Maybe he will when he gets released on bond."

"Hell, I'll bet the commissioners don't let him come near this place."

"You may be right, but you can handle things on your own. It looks as if the burden is on you, that is, finishing up the Jeffries case. Are you up to it?"

"I think so. I'll concentrate on it, and when it's finished, they can have this place. I'm history."

"I don't blame you. I've given legal advice to you, Roy, Bob, and a friend at the DA's office. My saving grace is that these were consultations, and I don't actually represent any of you. I can't represent any of you if I'm a witness at the trial, that would disqualify me as your attorney."

"Micki, do I need an attorney?"

"Not the way I see it. Bob is the only one who needs an attorney." I had to admit I was secretly worried whether or not Roy was being totally honest about his involvement.

"I guess the feds will be showing up here pretty soon, huh?"

"I would imagine. Anna, I just heard something else disturbing at the courthouse. Someone told me that the DA is hiding some of the crime lab evidence from the feds."

"Who told you that?"

"A friend of mine, Alan. He's an assistant DA. He said they turned over everything except one large folder from the lab. And get this. It contains the missing bloody shoes and the fingerprint cards. They've been there all along, and the DA could have used them at the first trial, but he didn't. The question is, why not?"

"Why would he hold back evidence that would help get him a conviction?"

"Same reason a DA would intentionally cause a mistrial."

"You think he did it on purpose?"

"That's how it looks. Why else would he inflame the jury to the extent that the judge declared a mistrial? He also overlooked critical evidence."

"What's his motive?"

"Politics and greed. Maybe Susan and Glen tried to buy him off or maybe someone promised him greatness if he would overlook certain evidence and lose the trial. He's always appeared stupid, so no one would doubt that he goofed up the trial. But he is powerful, and he has intelligent people working for him. It's not hard to overlook the fact that he's an idiot."

"I always believed that he fouled it up," she confessed.

"See what I mean."

"Micki, who's responsible for telling the feds about the DA's misconduct?"

"I hope I can talk Alan into doing it. Who knows? Maybe he'll get a promotion out of it."

"Let me get back to work. It sounds like my time here is limited."

"Sure, okay. I wanted to be the first one to tell you about Bob and the missing link in the chain of custody regarding the evidence."

"Now we know where everything is, or do we?"

"As much as we'll ever know. It was too much money for Susan to handle, and she spread the greed in too many different directions."

"I'll call you after the feds drop by."

"Please do. I want to be one step ahead of them."

I sat at my desk most of the afternoon and looked out the window. Events were about to break, no one was in control, and we would all be spun around like dust devils. I decided that sitting there was useless. I was going home. I picked up Michael from my folk's house, and we ate an early supper before the high school baseball game. At the game Michael got busy eating hotdogs and popcorn. I couldn't imagine where he put it all. Michael could name all the players, and their respective positions. He loved the game, and he couldn't wait until he was eight to begin his ascent to the big leagues.

He fell asleep in the car on the drive home. I could barely carry him into the house. He was growing so fast, and getting really heavy now. No bath or bedtime story tonight. I tucked him in and headed straight for the television to watch the ten o'clock news. No doubt that Bob would make his star appearance tonight. After a few commercials, the lead story aired. It wasn't about Bob at all. The anchor looked directly into the camera and announced the death of Sheriff Glen Harding and Susan Jeffries.

"They were found dead this evening around eight o'clock at the River's Inn downtown. While making his rounds, a watchman for the Inn noticed an open door on the back side of the Inn. The television was blaring loudly from inside the darkened room. He turned on the lights to investigate and found the naked bodies of Sheriff Harding and Ms. Susan Jeffries, widow of Wayne Jeffries. They were lying together, each had a shotgun wound to the head. Authorities say that the shots were fired from a .28 gauge shotgun. The widow Harding cannot be found for comment. An investigation is ongoing. Police have no suspects at this time."

I couldn't believe it. Who was left to kill them? Bob was still in jail, or was he? Wait, wait a minute. The newscaster had another story, this was the one I was expecting.

"Earlier today, Bob McNamara, Director of the Crime Laboratory, turned himself in to authorities for reasons unknown. We have little information from the district attorney's office or the police department. Officer LeRoy Roberts would only say, as he escorted Mr. McNamara to jail, that the arrest was in connection with an ongoing investigation. Mr. McNamara's attorney is not free to comment at this time. Mr. McNamara is in jail tonight, pending a bail hearing tomorrow at one o'clock."

Bingo, Bob was still in jail. If Susan and Glen were killing anyone who touched the Jeffries money, who killed them?

My phone rang almost immediately. It was Anna. "Micki, did you see the news?"

"Do you have any idea who killed our lovers? All my theories just went kaput."

"I thought Bob said Glen and Susan were the ones doing the killing, or having it done." Anna sounded confused.

"Maybe Bob lied. He's in protective custody tonight, and Sheriff Glen and his Buckeroo have gone to their permanent rodeo down under."

"Maybe Bob doesn't know who's in control. Jake was a liar, a thief, and a murderer. Why would Bob trust him?" She was always looking to find an out for Bob.

"We have a hinky situation here. Everyone tied to this case is dead now except—Bob, Roy, and the District Attorney. I'm convinced the DA's involved."

"Don't forget us, we're not dead yet. You and me."

"But we don't stand to benefit from the outcome of the case, not financially or politically." But Roy did.

"Where do we stand, Micki? I hope Bob doesn't try to implicate us in his cover-up. I'm scared."

"Me too. He's such a chickenshit. He may want company in his jail cell. But everything we know is secondhand, and that's not good enough."

"What about the missing evidence? Can't we tell the feds about that?"

"It's not our place. Someone from the DA's Office has to tell."

"I'll get my lab reports written up in the morning. When the FBI shows up, I'll be waiting for them."

"That's all you can do."

My call waiting started to beep. "Anna, let me call you back tomorrow. Les must be trying to call." I didn't want Les to hear any anxiety in my voice, so I answered cheerfully.

"You didn't watch the news, did you?" Roy joked.

"I damn sure did. I thought you were Les, and I was trying to sound normal. He doesn't like the idea of me running around playing cops and robbers."

"Well, we're back at square one. We can't believe anything Bob says. The two leading suspects are dead, and so is their hired gun, damn Jake's eyes."

"That's what I told Anna a few minutes ago, but she thinks Bob was telling all he knew. Roy, you need to check out the DA's office. They didn't turn over all the evidence to the feds in the Jeffries case."

"Where did you get an idea like that?"

"One of the assistants told me."

"Is he trustworthy?"

"Yes, and he's worried about his own ass. Mack held back evidence from the first trial, and the feds aren't aware of it."

"If Mack is involved in this deal, I'll find out about it." Roy sounded determined.

"Better find a suspect soon, Roy. We're the only ones left, and we don't have motives. With Jake, Susan, and Glen all dead, we're up a creek for answers."

"We'll get it done, and before the feds know what hit them."

"Somehow I thought there would be some salacious indictments handed down on Wednesday. Then Bob, Susan, and Glen would all be in the pokey together by the end of the day. Now it looks like Bob's butt is hanging out there all by itself."

"Don't fret, we're close. I can feel it. By the end of the week, all of this will be resolved and life will go on as usual."

I was wide-ass awake after those last two phone calls, so I called Les to calm my nerves.

He answered on the second ring,

"Hi, there. How was your flight?"

"Fine. It sure has been quiet here since Michael left. I miss you both. Good news though. I'll be home for good this weekend."

"Terrific. We'll hit the bookstore Saturday and plan our summer vacation. I can't wait."

"Neither can I. It seems like I've been gone for years rather than months."

"It's awful being completely alone—except for your work." I secretly wondered when he would leave again.

"What about the Jeffries case? Micki, it made the news here."

"Which part—the double murder or Bob turning himself in?"

"Both. Are they related?"

"I would imagine so."

"Who killed the sheriff and his girlfriend?"

"That's the question of the hour. The District Attorney's office made a big issue of the widow being unavailable for comment. That's what the news commentator said anyway."

"Do you think Harding's wife killed them?"

"Who's to say? I can't imagine that Glen's wife didn't suspect something years ago." I'd been wondering why she put up with it.

"It put our sleepy little town on the map. Now we look like a community of perverts. I hope we didn't make a mistake moving back. I only agreed so Michael could get to know his grandparents and grow up in a small town." I could hear the frustration in his voice. "Shit, that's four dead people associated with the Jeffries murder. You know how people from Colorado hate Texans. They'll all be talking about the floater in the septic tank, the vegematic murder, and now the pair of dead spooners. Only Wayne went with a touch of dignity, shot in the back diving under his desk trying to save his skin."

"You're being facetious, right?"

"Yes, I am."

"Les, more than likely I'll be forced to testify in any trial that comes up relevant to Wayne's murder. Maybe we can squeeze in our vacation first."

"Why do you have to testify?"

"I was the original chemist on the case, and I always get subpoenaed when the appeals courts remand the case back to the original trial court. Or, as in this case, when it resulted in a mistrial."

"God, will you ever get away from that work? You've been subpoenaed for something or other since the day I met you."

"I don't know. There's no statute of limitations on murder cases in this state."

"Great, that makes me feel a lot better."

"Sorry, but just as I think I'm out, they pull me back in." I used my best godfather voice.

He laughed, but I could tell the situation did not please him. It was all right for him to be gone months at a time doing whatever he felt was necessary for his career. But it wasn't acceptable when my work kept me away from him. It was something we would have to work out when he finally came home. I had been alone a good while, and his coming home would be an adjustment for me.

"You better get some rest. I know you're working two jobs. Why I'll never understand, but it's your business."

"I'm taking care of my friends and finishing what I started. It's hard to detach myself from this case since I was there from the beginning. Don't make light of it. It's important to me."

"I know, I love you."

"Love you too. Good night."

Les avoided conflict at all costs. We fought very little. It takes two to tango. At least he accepted me for who I was, and he didn't try to change me. It was the closest I had ever come to unconditional love.

Chapter Twenty-Seven

*S*leep, how would that be possible? I thought maybe I'd take one of those sleeping pills the doctor gave me when I had surgery. I never took any of them then, but I'd need some sleep if my intuition was on target. We were all in for a roller-coaster ride. I slept for about four hours. I didn't feel great, but it was better than no sleep at all. Once I dropped Michael at school, I went straight to the courthouse to see if there were any new developments. First I stopped to see Alan.

"Talk to the feds yet?"

"No, I'm chicken."

"You better get right with them or you may be a dead chicken. Or at best a roasted one."

"Don't scare me like that."

"I'm trying to get you to do what you have to."

"Micki, they're handing down the indictments on Bob today, a lot of them."

"What is there besides concealing or destroying evidence?"

"Murder of Jake Edmonds, official oppression, illegal wiretapping, and misprision. I don't even know what misprision is. Mack left state court this morning and headed for the federal courthouse bright and early. That's the news he brought back to the office. One more piece of news. They indicted Mrs. Harding for the double murder of her husband and Susan Jeffries."

"Feds didn't waste any time, did they? What a rocket docket. One day you're a suspect, and the next day you're indicted. Scary system, I've never liked it. What clued them in that the widow killed her husband and his lover?" Convenient timing for whoever has access to Wayne's insurance money, I thought.

"Eyewitness, someone called Crimestoppers."

"Seems sad doesn't it? She has those kids to raise by herself, and now she faces prison. Who'll get the kids?"

"She should have thought about that before she killed those two."

"You think like a prosecutor. Don't you ever think like a human being? She was a victim before they became her victims. Besides, what happened to innocent until proven guilty? Why would she kill him now? Mrs. Harding must have known about the affair for years."

"I guess I do feel bad for her. I mean, I feel bad for the kids. She's guilty, Micki. They always are."

"When are the arraignments in her case and Bob's set?"

"You mean bond hearings, don't you?"

"No, I'm not interested in those. There won't be any bail in Bob's case or the widow's, you know the feds."

"Arraignments have been expedited. Bond hearings are this afternoon at one, and arraignments in the morning at nine. How did you know they would be expedited?"

"I've been to federal court a few times."

"That's right, your big cocaine defendant."

"And don't forget my big embezzler."

"Yeah, you bitched about those cases for years."

"If you had a federal license, you'd have something to bitch about too."

"Poor Micki." He was rubbing his fingers back and forth like a little violin.

"Fuck you." This brought on more laughter from him. "I hope you're still laughing when they indict your whole office."

"Do you know something I don't?" The smile left his face.

"Maybe."

"Don't jack me around. You know we're all worried."

"Who's 'we'?"

"The whole goddamn office. We know about Mack's wiretapping of the sheriff's office—and anyone else he felt like listening in on."

"What wiretapping? I thought you were referring to secreting evidence in a murder case."

"Hell, that's small potatoes for an ambitious guy like Mack. He even bugged the crime lab. I think he and Bob and Glen had some elaborate blackmail scheme going."

"How do you know?"

"I came across some tapes and did some listening after-hours, when everyone else had gone home. I even took some to my house. I told a few people here, and they told others, and now the whole fucking office knows. Mack doesn't know we know. I almost wish someone would speak up. I just knew one of the mouthier secretaries would have said something by now, but everyone is afraid. It's like if we don't talk about it, it doesn't exist."

"What kind of conversations are on the tapes?"

"A few of your conversations are taped, Micki. Nothing incriminating. You and your mother, you and your husband, nothing interesting."

"That sucks. I thought the FBI bugged my house."

Alan went on. "It's hours and hours of everyone here in the office. You know how paranoid we all are. The most disturbing conversations are Mack's with Bob.

Even worse are Mack's with Glen. I didn't get the entire scenario. But I listened to more than enough to know that people were getting in the way of an elaborate scheme of blackmail—and then people started to die. I didn't know what to do."

"You better talk to Roy, and then you better debrief with the feds. Your life is in jeopardy if you know this much."

"I thought that I was safe since Glen is dead and Bob is in jail. I don't know if I want to place my life and career in the hands of Roy Roberts. I've heard he'll do anything to move up in the department. He scares me almost as much as Mack."

I didn't like hearing that, but there was nothing I could say.

"You're sitting here under the nose of a criminal, I guarantee that. Mack is greedier, more ambitious, and sleazier than the dead parties to this conspiracy. Don't let him fool you. He may look stupid in trial and appear uninformed about most of your case work, but he's not interested in that part of his job. His interests lie in what the DA's office can bring him down the line, like power and position. He has no conscience. He'll have you killed, same as the others, if you don't get out of here. The feds won't take kindly to your story if someone else tells it before you do. Roy is the least of your worries. You could go down with Mack, if for nothing else, for misprision. The feds could care less about any of you. They want convictions, and there is virtually no probation in the federal system these days. Almost everyone, even first offenders, get federal prison sentences." I paused for a moment after my filibuster, for effect. Alan was stunned, absolutely flabbergasted at the mere idea that he could go to prison. I could see the fear in his eyes.

"What's misprision?"

"You're interested now that it pertains to you, huh? You'd know the answer to that question if you had a federal license."

"Don't be a wiseass."

"It means that you knew about the occurrence of a crime, and you did nothing to stop it. Nor did you notify the authorities that you knew an offense had been committed, or was about to be committed."

"That's a federal crime?"

"Yes. There's no equivalent in the state system. That's why you're unfamiliar with the statute. If my gut feelings are accurate, the next twenty-four hours are crucial. What are you going to do?"

He hesitated, then mustered a response. "I'll talk to Roy and then talk to the feds. I'm only doing this because Roy's the lead investigator. I know you have to start at the bottom of the chain of command when negotiating with the feds."

"I'll call Roy now. Where do you want to meet him?"

"Out in front of the federal courthouse. Might as well get it over with. It'll take me several hours to satisfy their curiosity."

"Keep Roy by your side. He's your golden goose. Discuss

the issue of your immunity from prosecution before you utter a word to them. Don't take a lawyer—you're a prosecutor. They'll feel a certain camaraderie toward you. You know how to protect your own penal interests. Discuss both testimonial and transactional immunity. Don't let them trick fuck you. I need to tell you one more thing. I'm asking you to trust Roy because he can corroborate the DA's blackmail scheme."

"Thanks. I'll be in touch. Don't call me here. I'll be taking an administrative leave of absence until this mess is resolved."

"Ask for protection. We don't know how far Mack's reach is, and you don't want him to reach out and touch you with his lethal hand."

"I wish I had talked to you about this earlier, Micki, but I wasn't aware that you were working on the case."

"Nobody knew. I don't think that you're too late. Everything will be all right. I'm leaving now, and when I'm out of the building, leave behind me. Mail your letter of leave of absence. Don't stay and type it out."

I left quickly, and when I had my office in sight, I paged Roy. He returned my page immediately.

"Micki, what's up?"

"Got some late-breaking news for you, and an assignment. Alan Griffith with the DA's office has some information for you regarding Mack and some illegal wiretapping. Both the DA's office and the sheriff's office have been wired for sound. There are also some interesting conversations between Mack, Bob, and the late sheriff."

"Finally, the case breaks, and you would be the one closest to it. I'm jealous. What's my assignment?"

"Meet with Alan, take notes, and then accompany him to the federal prosecutor's office. Don't leave him under any circumstances, record everything that is said between him and the feds, and get him some protection. He'll be waiting for you in front of the federal courthouse in thirty minutes. Can you make it?"

"Anything else?"

"That's all you'll have time for today. I'll take care of the rest."

"You won't be playing cop, will you?"

"Don't be jealous, and don't worry about me. Do your job and get your name on the evening news."

"My pleasure. I'll be in touch."

By now, I was sitting at my desk calling Anna.

"Crime Lab."

"Why are you answering the phone?"

"The secretary is out, and the lab technician quit again today."

"We have a break in the case, Anna. Before I get into it, how much money did you find out at Belle?"

"Right at four hundred thousand dollars."

"Gee, why didn't you tell me sooner?"

"I just got around to counting it last night before I wrote up my lab reports. Why do you ask?"

"Remember the amount Bob was supposed to receive from Jake?"

"Five hundred thousand. I see what you're thinking. Bob lied when he told Roy that he never got the money. I bet he kept some with him. That's what he ran away on, the hundred thousand. Then he stashed the rest at Belle. Once Belle made the crime scene circuit, he was afraid to go get it."

"That's about the size of it. Why did he lie about being paid and give us that story about Jake being afraid of Susan and Glen?"

"I bet he set us up. He used us to get what he wanted—money and escape from prosecution. I bet he has a lot more money hidden out. I'm going to check out his beach cabin and see what I can find. He's in jail, it can't hurt. We covered Belle from stem to stern. I think we got everything relevant to Wayne's case, and a lot that wasn't."

"Set up is right, Anna. But don't go to the cabin without Roy and me. We have our illustrious DA strutting around at present, but he's going down as we speak. One of his assistants is at the courthouse making the fed's day and their case. They couldn't find their butts with both hands. It's pitiful really. It took you, me, and a cop to solve their big conspiracy. Well, almost solve—we don't have all the details yet, but soon, very soon."

"What should I do with my reports?"

"Get Roy to deliver them to the feds. Call him tomorrow, he's tied up today. God, I almost forgot to tell you. They've charged

Bob with Jake's murder—and wiretapping, official oppression, and misprision."

"No! They charged him with murder?"

"Yep, and a lot of other piddly stuff."

"Good idea regarding the lab reports. Head the feds off at the pass. Then I won't have to deal with them until trial time."

"I need to go practice some law. A reminder, do not go to the cabin alone. If you get the urge, count the dead bodies: one, two, three, four, five."

"We'll go together, maybe tomorrow night."

"Good. Maybe the DA will be behind bars by then."

For the life of me I couldn't concentrate on the divorce case that I was working on. Images of Alan and Roy at the federal courthouse kept buzzing through my mind. I was dying to know what new information, if any, the feds got from Alan.

It was a fact that the FBI had been contacted by now. Someone from their local office was sitting there with the federal prosecutor and my friends. I hoped Roy called soon. The morning seemed never-ending. After lunch it was even worse. We were covered up with initial conferences of would-be clients all afternoon. I tried to listen attentively to the potential clients and take good notes, but my mind and my heart were not in it. Finally, about four o'clock, Roy called.

"Six fucking hours. Those bastards don't do anything fast. I can't sit still that long." I ignored his complaints.

"How did Alan do?"

"Like a champ. They loved him. Said he'd get immunity. They weren't looking to prosecute him or anyone in his office. Just Mack the Knife. That's what they call him since Jake was murdered."

"Oh, yuk. Did Alan reveal anymore tidbits?"

"Nope."

"I'm relieved to hear that. Criminal clients always leave out the important information, and you find out about it too late. That's what I am used to, trial by ambush. At least Alan told me the truth."

"There is the big question. Who is the mastermind in the blackmail scheme, Bob or Mack? The feds believe that, when push comes to shove, they'll turn on each other."

Roy and I talked for over an hour. We ran hypotheticals by each other and discussed various scenarios involving the two suspects. Finally, I remembered Anna's suggestion, and I mentioned it to Roy.

"Roy, what about searching Bob's beach cabin for more clues? Anna thought it would be a good idea. Can you get a search warrant this late? It's five o'clock now."

"I'll see if any of the district judges are still around. It's a trial week, and some of them run late with their cases. I was in court until six yesterday testifying in a robbery case. If no one is around, I'll call one of them at home. Want to go with us tonight?"

"Is the Pope Catholic?"

"I think so." He stammered.

"What time? I'll need to arrange for a sitter for Michael."

"Should be ready to roll before eight. How about it?"

"Do you think it'll be safe?"

"Unless Mack has the place staked out."

"I'll call Anna and tell her. The ballistics at Belle gave her good information, but the trace evidence was mostly related to Bob's sleazy side jobs.

"What a jerk. Let's ride together in one car. I don't want a parking lot down at the beach cabin."

"We'll meet you at the stadium parking lot by seven-thirty."

"See you then."

Sherry had already left while I was on the phone talking to Roy. I packed up my briefcase and left. Tomorrow morning I planned to be in federal court when they arraigned Bob and the widow Harding. I wanted to see the look on Bob's face when they read the charges to him. He was expecting the charge of concealing and tampering with evidence. A murder charge, his connection to Mack, and the wiretapping should scare him shitless. That's saying a lot since he's full of it. I pitied Mrs. Harding. I was not looking forward to seeing her grief-stricken face. I hoped none of her children were there.

I picked up Michael from my folks and took him home for a few hours. He would be disappointed if I left him with a sitter. Maybe Jean would entertain him for me. I couldn't ask mom.

She'd ask too many questions.

"Jean, could you watch Michael for a couple of hours?"

"Now?"

"I could drop him off about seven."

"Sure. Got a hot date?" Jean enjoyed spending time with Michael.

"Be serious. I'm working on the mystery case."

"Be careful. All those dead people are in the news."

"How's your arm healing?"

"Peachy. Guess I had a dangerous occupation myself for awhile, but that's all over now. It's back to teaching for me."

"Since you brought up your last job, the tail we had on the way to Shelby was that crazy woman. Another thing: she was my so-called burglar. One evening she followed Anna and me. She thought it was you and me, and trashed Anna's house as well. She was a little confused."

"I wish you'd hit her when you took those shots," Jean said flatly. "I feel guilty for saying that, but I'm trying to be more hard-hearted so I won't feel so scared."

"She didn't scare easily. I guess that's why they call her crazy."

"Bring Michael over. Will you be late? Can he spend the night?"

"I don't think so. I need to be at the federal courthouse early in the morning anyway, so I'll be back by eleven or so." I knew Jean would let Michael stay up all night if I let him spend the night. After Michael and I had supper, I gave him his bath, put him in his pajamas, and left him at Jean's.

Roy was waiting for us when we arrived at the stadium. There was a baseball game in progress across the street. As we got into Roy's undercover car, I was beginning to wish we were here for the game rather than a trip to the beach.

I thought about Les and remembered I hadn't called him. Michael and I were his only family. His parents had died years ago, and he didn't have any brothers or sisters. I reached for my digital phone and gave him a call. I pretended I was at home. There was no way I could confess what I was about to do. It was a relief when Les didn't ask me any questions. I told him Michael and I were fine, and we would talk to him tomorrow night. Anna and Roy were both quiet while I was talking. Only the judge who signed the warrant knew where we were. Supposedly Anna and I were going to collect evidence from the cabin.

Chapter Twenty-Eight

The cabin was about thirty minutes from the stadium. Not one of us spoke for the last fifteen minutes. We were all dreading what we might find. When we arrived, it was pitch dark. There was no moon.

Anna led the way. She had been there before. Bob had her run errands to and from the cabin when he was on vacation, which was often. We carried no gear, and Roy had to pick the lock. There were no lights on inside, and it was spookier than hell. I could hear the Gulf breeze blowing across the sand, and waves breaking on the shore. I couldn't see the water, but I knew it was as dark as copper pennies.

Roy went in first, then Anna. I was last. We all stood there for a few seconds, afraid to breathe, trying to see in the darkness. It was useless, I couldn't see my own hand in front of my face. I nudged Roy, so he would turn on his flashlight. We heard movement coming from a bedroom in the back. It was obvious we were standing in the kitchen. We all froze. Roy placed a finger over his mouth. Anna and I moved back toward the door in case we had to make a run for it. Roy tiptoed across the kitchen, leaned forward, took his gun from his boot, and cocked it, all without making a sound. Anna and I looked at each other and then back at

Roy. He opened a bedroom door and turned on a light. At that very moment we heard a gunshot. We ran to the back of the cabin to find Roy face-to-face with Bob.

"What the hell are you doing here?" Bob demanded.

"I should ask you the same question." Roy said.

"We have a warrant to search the place." Anna spoke up.

"How did you get out of jail?" I asked.

"You almost shot me, Bob." Roy complained.

The bullet had lodged in the door frame. Bob was not any kind of marksman. Fortunately, Roy hadn't returned the kindness.

"What the hell are you doing here?" Anna glared at her boss. Running the lab by herself had taken its toll on her.

Bob stood there, looking at us for a few seconds. "I'm not out on bond if that's what you're all thinking. It'll be all over the news by tomorrow morning anyway—after the arraignments, that is."

"Fill us in, dirtbag," Roy chided.

"Before you judge me, let me tell you what has happened. It all began when Jake Edmonds approached me to conceal certain evidence in the Jeffries trial. You all think I sold out for five hundred thousand dollars. That's what the Texas Rangers wanted everyone to think. They began investigating this case thirteen years ago, when I approached them about my meeting with Jake—and the phone call I received from the District Attorney. The Rangers knew that Mack was dirty, and they had more than once set a trap for him. But every time they did, he slipped away. He insulated himself with powerful people. I know you all think he's dumb and dirty, but let me tell you, he's an evil megalomaniac. He scares me to death. And four people are dead because of him, not counting Wayne Jeffries of course."

"What about the missing evidence? You're the one who concealed it, aren't you?" Roy sounded confused, and angry.

"No, I let Jake think I was concealing it, when I actually turned it over to the DA's office. It was Mack's choice to eliminate it from the first trial. Mack thought we were partners in crime, concealing the bloody shoes and fingerprint evidence. This is when the Rangers really began to watch him. Well, nothing much happened for awhile, and Mack never prosecuted Jake for the west end burglaries. No one but the DA's office had the evidence to prove them. So Jake thought that he was off the hook, but he wasn't, not with Mack anyway. Glen and Susan told Mack about Jake's demand for more money, and Mack had him killed. Jake was blackmailing me until the day he died. Even Mack believed that I helped him conceal or destroy state evidence. So then it was down to Susan, Glen, Mack, and me."

I interrupted him, "Where and when did Mack enter into the blackmail scheme? It's apparent when you became involved, but I don't understand the sequence of events."

"After Susan solicited Jake to murder her husband, Sheriff Harding went along with it. He wanted Susan and all the money. After all, he didn't have to get his hands dirty. Later on, Mack had Billy Shipley killed when Glen told him that the rookie was getting too close to the truth. I didn't know about Billy's murder until recently. Glen concocted a story about him taking an under-cover position with the Drug Enforcement Agency.

"By this time, Glen was aware that Mack had the whole floor of the sheriff's office wired for sound, wiretapping all the way. It became readily apparent when Mack showed up at the no-tell motel where Susan and Glen met each week. Mack made it per-fectly clear to Susan and Glen that he knew about the murder for hire and about Wayne's insurance death benefits. He wanted five million dollars from Susan—or she, Glen, and Jake would spend the rest of their lives in prison. He even threatened to seek the death penalty. I think at first macho Sheriff Glenny thought that he could do battle with the Mack, but it became obvious to him that he was no match for the DA. Mack sent Glen over to check the body of Billy Shipley at Belle, hide the nine millimeter used to kill him, hide the original trial transcripts, and leave a five hun-dred thousand dollar installment on the five million he requested. He didn't want the full amount yet, just a little to tide him over until the smoke settled on the Jeffries case. Mack thought he had me under control, and he waited years to collect his money. He smelled the feds when they came around. He knew the Rangers were investigating some aspects of the Jeffries case. He was slick enough and patient enough to wait it out. He forced Susan to place most of the insurance money in various accounts in Switzerland and the Caymans. The money Anna collected at

Belle was Mack's first installment, minus the hundred thousand dollars he had already removed. He left the money at Belle for safekeeping until he took his vacation out of the country this summer. Only Anna got to it before he could.

"At some point Mack thought the feds and the Rangers had abandoned the investigation. That's when he started making mistakes. Mack sent Susan a drop dead letter from his office, meaning that he had closed the Jeffries case due to insufficient evidence. In his mind it was all over. He thought the feds and the Rangers had lost interest in the case. He had no idea that they were investigating him." Bob paused.

Roy asked a question. "What about your prostitution and porn activities out there at Belle?"

"It was Mack. He loved hookers, thrived on them, and used them frequently. He also had a weakness for porn and S&M. He used my place, and I hated him for it. The Rangers convinced me to allow it for awhile. I never went out there when that was going on, but I had hopes of retiring there someday. I didn't want the place ransacked and demolished by a bunch of sick perverts.

"It started several months ago. Mack kept his activities elsewhere until Glen told him about my place. Glen mentioned it one evening at a party, when he still thought that he and Mack were friends. I wish I could have seen the look on Glen's face when he realized who his nemesis really was. Mack didn't approach me about Belle for awhile, but when his other arrangements fizzled out, he figured that since he was blackmailing me with the Jeffries case, he might as well take further advantage of my pathetic situation. He had all of the taped conversations between Glen and Jake, Susan and Jake, Susan and Glen, Jake and me, you name it. He spent a lot of time eavesdropping.

"I'm not a significant character in this play, but Mack thinks I am. He knew that Jake confided in me, and killing Jake was unimportant to him. Jake was a criminal, a petty thief, and no one would miss him. Mack was crazy when he hired a professional and had Glen and Susan killed."

"I thought Glen's wife killed them?" said Roy.

"That's what Mack wanted everyone to think. He couldn't face the heat on that one. Killing the sheriff would bring in the cavalry. He paid a motel employee to lie for him and say she saw the wife's car in the parking lot. Even gave her license plate number. I think that's what he did with the hundred thousand dollars he had squirreled away. He paid the alleged eyewitness and the professional hit man. Billy was one thing, no one missed him. He had no family, except that sister in Florida. Jake was a petty criminal, and the police thought one of his former cell mates killed him. After all, he had spent time in prison. But Sheriff Glen, now that was another story. Mack has simply lost his mind and his tolerance for the situation. He had Glen and Susan killed to cover his tracks and keep all of the insurance money."

"What's going to happen at your arraignment tomorrow?" I asked.

"It will be a mock arraignment for the purpose of bringing Mack around. They'll arrest Mack when he shows up at my arraignment, which he will. There were never any charges filed against me. It was all a sham to bring Mack down. They targeted the heat in my direction to throw him off, let him relax, get sloppy. And he did.

"Alan Griffith, one of his assistants, turned him into the feds. Alan picked up on some tapes, some secreted evidence and some fabricated evidence. The Rangers were also able to pressure the alleged eyewitness in the sheriff's murder to finger Mack, who paid her to lie."

"What's weird about this deal, Bob, is the fact that the feds and the Rangers never went after Susan, Glen, and Jake, when they had them for conspiracy to murder, and for murder." Anna was angry and confused about Wayne's murder.

"Well, it's not strange, if you think of it in terms of an investigation. You see, the feds learned early on that the DA was involved in a clandestine association with the suspects, when he did a lay-down at the first trial. Contrary to popular belief, the man's not stupid in all respects. He took the case out of the hands of the judge and the jury when he intentionally caused a mistrial. But these things are harder to prove in reality than they are in theory. The judge contacted the feds after the trial, but it was too late. The evidence was disappearing. No one knew of Mack's involvement in the blackmail scheme until after the trial."

"How did Mack know about all of the insurance money before the trial?" Anna asked.

"He knew about the insurance proceeds, Jake's burglaries, Susan's law enforcement lover, the contract on Wayne's life, and every intimate conversation between Glen and Susan. All compliments of his wiretapping and his legal ability to compel information through the subpoena process. In this county, the District Attorney is the most powerful political figure. The office has a tremendous amount of power and prestige. The DA can accomplish things that the ordinary citizen cannot. His resources are unlimited, and he's protected and insulated to the point that it has taken years to bring Mack down. And we haven't done it yet. But Mack's downfall is his enormous ego. He had the audacity to wiretap his own telephone conversations. His mistake was believing that no one could touch him."

"What about tomorrow? Are they going to arrest him at your hearing?" I asked.

"Hopefully. A list of sealed indictments have come down with his name on them. A special grand jury sat at an unknown location Monday morning when I turned myself in. I was a decoy to attract Mack's attention, to preoccupy his curious mind while the grand jury sat. The feds wanted no hint of the federal charges in process getting back to Mack. He has spies and corrupt protectors everywhere. The grand jury heard only a portion of the evidence against Mack on Monday. They'll reconvene, once he's behind bars, to hear the rest of the evidence. It'll take weeks, maybe months, before the grand jury hears sufficient evidence to determine whether or not there will be further indictments. The feds didn't want to risk weeks of proceedings and the possibility of a leak to Mack. They were afraid that with all of those millions at his disposal, he'd rabbit out of the country, have a little plastic surgery, and never be seen again."

"Why hasn't he tried to kill you, Bob?" Roy knew he was the only investigator in the original murder case. Bob faked the threats and blackmail scheme toward Roy to keep him quiet. Bob knew Roy would investigate the case to death, so to speak.

"As far as he knew, I was blackmail material. Jake had told him so, and he mistakenly believed Jake. I never asked for money after the cover-up. I dealt with assistants when we went to trial on cases, and avoided Mack as much as possible. Besides, killing me would have been high profile, and he couldn't risk it. Billy and Jake were disposable, I wasn't. But now he's lost it. I wouldn't be surprised if he tried to kill me too.

"The Rangers wanted to place me in protective custody, but I felt safer out here. I don't trust anyone. It's like a godfather and his family of freaks. A lot of heads will roll before Mack sees his day in court."

Anna spoke softly at first, then her voice rose. "I'm sorry I thought you were such a bad man, but you've treated Micki and me like shit."

I couldn't apologize. I didn't like him, never had, never would, no matter what. Why should we believe this incredible tale? I wouldn't, not until the feds or the Rangers proved it to me. Yes, sir, the fat lady would have to sing before I bought into this grim fairytale. It seemed he had all of the answers, but we didn't even know the questions, so, hey—I was in a wait-and-see mode.

Roy didn't apologize either. Bob looked at us after Anna's apology. He had a question on his face. Neither of us said anything.

"Bob, I got a search warrant based on what I believe to be probable cause, and if you will step aside, I will conduct that search. Ladies, if you will, wait with Bob until I finish."

We both nodded, and Bob threw up his hands in desperation. Two hours later and empty-handed, we were homeward bound. Being out there gave me the creeps. Michael was fast asleep. I drove him home and carried his lead-weight little body to his bed again. It was ten-thirty.

Bad dreams were upon me all night long. My subconscious would not accept the fact that Bob had done the right thing and approached the feds when Jake first came to him. I didn't think he had it in him, and I had played right into his little covert operation. I was more comfortable in my belief that he was a criminal. I even believed the bullshit story he unfolded in my office just days ago.

I was afraid that I would oversleep, so I set the alarm to make the nine o'clock arraignment. I rushed Michael off to school, and then drove to my office. I left Sherry a note and promised to be back in two hours. Every form of law enforcement was present; city, county, state, federal, and their marked cars hogged the federal courthouse parking lot. I parked at the bank and walked across the street.

Chapter Twenty-Nine

As I entered the federal courthouse I was funneled through a metal detector and then into the already overcrowded courtroom. It brought back stressful memories. When the federal judge called your case, you walked through a pair of swinging gates about thigh high and stood before him. The bailiff customarily called the cases, and the announcement was, "The United States of America versus Duddly Dipshit." That is usually how I felt anyway. It was the whole United States of America versus your poor pitiful client and you. I never escaped the overwhelming feeling of being outnumbered in federal court. The odds were stacked against you from the beginning.

I wondered what the feds would charge old Mack with? Being here made me nervous, but I wasn't leaving. Not until I knew this case was headed for justice. It had been a long time getting here, and too many people had suffered and died along the way. Mack was in the front row, front and center so he had a good view of the proceedings. Mrs. Harding's family was present, her parents, children, and friends, the whole clan. Roy came in and sat next to me as I was looking over the crowd. It felt reassuring having him there, although I still felt uneasy about my feelings for him. I got a panic attack every time I thought about

Les finding out about my indiscretion. Two Texas Rangers, the chief of police, the mayor, several county court and district judges were present. The FBI had a few suits loitering about accomplishing nothing, as usual. The audience was unusually quiet for a crowd of that size.

"All rise," the bailiff shouted. We all stood while the federal judge took the bench. It was Judge Knowles, the biggest federal hard-ass of all federal judges in the State. Lucky Mack!

"The United States of America versus Robert McNamara," the bailiff stated with authority.

Judge Knowles: "Mr. McNamara, thank you for your cooperation. You are free to leave." The crowd gasped. There was whispering and a lot of nodding from the spectators.

"The United States of America versus Glenda Harding."

Judge Knowles: "Mrs. Harding, I am sorry for your loss and apologize for any humiliation you and your family may have experienced. You too are free to leave."

The crowd was gawking and groaning, and the bailiff had to calm them down. No one seemed to know what was going on. Watching Mack's face during the last two make-believe arraignments was hysterical. He was trying to appear unaffected by the proceedings, but he didn't have a poker face, no way he could hide his emotions. Roy stared him down through the entire proceeding. Four armed federal marshals approached Mack sitting in the front row with other dignitaries, and asked him to rise.

"What is the meaning of this?" he demanded.

"Mr. District Attorney," the federal judge addressed him with sarcasm. "You are to remain quiet and allow these men to handcuff you."

This was all geared to humiliate Mack in front of his friends and most of the law enforcement community. Once he was cuffed, the judge requested that he remain standing.

"Mr. District Attorney, a special grand jury has had the undesirable privilege of convening to investigate you and your official misconduct, which includes murder, the most hideous and lascivious of crimes. Please remain standing while all of the indictments are read out loud to you by the United States Attorney, Mrs.

Price. You may enter your plea to the indictments after each one is read out loud."

Mack only nodded. He was doomed, and he knew it. Eric Clapton's "I Shot the Sheriff" was buzzing through my head as the charges were read.

After the preliminary legalese, the prosecutor got to the meat of the indictment: "Conspiracy to commit murder in the first degree of Billy Shipley, conspiracy to commit murder in the first degree of Jake Edmonds, conspiracy to commit murder in the first degree of Glen Harding, and conspiracy to commit murder in the first degree of Susan Jeffries."

Next came so many wiretapping charges that I lost count. Then came the pornography, prostitution, and drug charges. These too were numerous. Lastly, were counts of official oppression, prosecutorial misconduct, misprision, and securities fraud.

Mr. District Attorney, as the judge referred to him, was pleading "Not Guilty" to each and every charge. I bet it took thirty minutes for all of the charges to be read and another thirty minutes before all of Mack's pleas were entered. No attorney in town would touch this. The political and social implications were too great. Mack would have to resort to out-of-town counsel. He'd never plead to any of the charges. It would offend his sensibilities to do the right thing and just plead guilty. He would spend the taxpayer's money and prolong the agony with trial after trial. I couldn't help wondering who he would take down with him. Roy? Alan? Anna? Me? I hoped not.

"Mr. District Attorney." The judge liked ridiculing his title. "You are to be held without bail. Pretrial motions are due in each case in ten days, without delay. Your first trial date is ninety days from today's date, and there will be no continuances. In the event that future indictments are handed down by the grand jury, I will set a time line for each subsequent case. Mrs. Thibodeaux, read him the Miranda warning." With that Mack was ushered out of the courtroom to his federal jail cell.

For a moment, everyone sat stunned in their seats, and then, little by little, they left the courtroom. Anna was working. Too bad she couldn't be here, but duty called. I knew she would like the closure she got in her friend's death. I needed to call her when I got to the car. Roy had been unusually quiet during the proceedings, and he walked me to my car. He turned to me and said, "Micki, the governor has asked me to step in as acting sheriff. What do you think?"

"Well, it means switching sides. Is it better to be chief of police or sheriff?"

"One's as good as the other, I guess." He shrugged.

"I think it's wonderful. You can run for reelection when Glen's term is up. It's what you've always wanted. The only difference is that you will be a county servant rather than a city servant. Will you be considered a traitor for leaving the police department?"

"I don't think so. I believe it'll promote good working relations between the two departments. I'll always be loyal to the guys at the department."

"That's all they can ask of you. You always wanted to be a big shot. Here's your chance. Go for it."

"If I can't have you, I may as well be sheriff. It'll keep me busy."

"I'm already spoken for, Roy, but I'll take that as a compliment. I wish you the best. I'm sure there is a Mrs. Sheriff out there somewhere waiting for you. Don't give up."

He kissed me lightly on the lips, gave me a charming smile, and walked to his police car. Things had turned out well for him, and he would finally have the respect and position he had yearned for all these years. He was young and ambitious when I met him, and he had grown and matured since then. The publicity of the arrest, numerous indictments, and the subsequent prosecution of the District Attorney would bring him instant admiration and fame. Then I remembered the phone call I had promised to make.

Anna answered the phone at the lab, and we agreed to meet for lunch at the Boondocks. I drove back to my office and phoned Les and told him the news. His voice showed a hint of relief, and he had some great news for me as well. He would be home on Friday, just two days from now, with our travel arrangements to Italy in hand. We were leaving in twenty-one days for Europe.

Before lunch Sherry and I went through my cases so we could determine what would get accomplished during the next three weeks. Then I left for lunch to tell Anna all about the morning's proceedings. I explained what happened in court, and then she showed me her letter of resignation and retirement. Bob had come back to the office ready and willing to work as director again, but she had a little surprise for him. It was long overdue, and she would enjoy her life now. She and her husband were taking a group motorcycle trip to Canada before Harry started another marijuana eradication program in East Texas. I was happy for her, and I told her about my plans to travel to Italy this summer with Les and Michael.

"Life will be peaceful, won't it, Anna?"

"I'm looking forward to it." We walked arm in arm to our cars. When we left each other there were tears in our eyes.

Driving back to the office I caught the end of a news bulletin. Assistant District Attorney Alan Griffith, would be acting district attorney until the November election.

I called Jean to tell her life was good again and to invite her to open a bottle of wine with me to celebrate. She was ecstatic but asked if she could have a ride to the airport instead.

"Where you going?" I asked.

"To New York City!"

"Without me?"

"I'm sorry, Micki. I need to take a vacation now. I'm teaching this summer. Please take me to the airport."

"Okay, okay. We'll go together before Christmas, and shop and see the gorgeous lights."

"Great." She sounded so happy.

At the airport I left Jean in front, where the porters checked her baggage. She waved good-bye. Jean was flying out of state and Anna was moving away. I was alone again, but not for long. Les was coming home. That made me smile.

About four that afternoon, Jean called from La Guardia. She had just seen Roy boarding a plane for Switzerland. He was dressed up like what we teasingly referred to as a drug courier: dark sunglasses, black silk shirt, black slacks, black lizard shoes with matching belt, and last but most importantly, a big flashy diamond ring. Roy hadn't seen Jean, but she'd seen him. Maybe it was Roy, not Bob, who needed the bayou privilege. With all my heart I hoped he was just flying out of the country to bring back Wayne's insurance money.

Dallari Lynne Landry is a native Texan. She grew up reading mysteries and poetry as a child, and wrote her first story when she was nine. Her degree in Biology and minor in Chemistry came in handy when she was a chemist-toxicologist with the Jefferson County Regional Crime Lab in Beaumont. Testifying as an expert witness and dealing with the legal aspects of her cases enticed her into attending St. Mary's University School of Law in San Antonio. Presently, she practices criminal defense and does family law mediations in the Texas Hill Country. Dallari hopes to draw on her knowledge of the law and forensic science in more novels featuring Micki Lane. She lives in a small town a lot like Liberty with her husband and their son.